SEARCHING FOR MARILYN MONROE

Parables and other Animals

SEARCHING FOR
MARILYN MONROE

Parables and other Animals

Pae Veo

Illustrated by Derek Boe

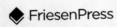 FriesenPress

Suite 300 - 990 Fort St
Victoria, BC, V8V 3K2
Canada

www.friesenpress.com

ISBN
978-1-5255-2347-2 (Hardcover)
978-1-5255-2348-9 (Paperback)
978-1-5255-2349-6 (eBook)

1. FICTION

Distributed to the trade by The Ingram Book Company

TABLE OF CONTENTS

ANIMALS

||||||||||||||||||||||||||||||||||||||||||||||||||||||||||||||||||||||||||||||||

A man sat alone in a room filled with one thousand lit candles,
until one by one they all went out.

||||||||||||||||||||||||||||||||||||||||||||||||||||||||||||||||||||||||||||||||

STORIES

SEARCHING FOR
MARILYN MONROE

My life is a rather grim one,
One day I shall perhaps describe it to you in great detail.

—*John Kennedy Toole*

PART ONE

Beyond the isles around the Mississippi, US 90, and the short trek of eighty-five miles off New Orleans' borders, past Pearlington, Waveland, onward towards the Gulf Coast and resting at Biloxi was the inquisitive notebook on the dashboard of an abandoned vehicle. Folded between the seams of a notebook was an article that was dated August 5th, 1962. *Above the crisis, ninety miles off the coast of Florida, there lay a heavier burden that stole away some purity after overdosing on sleeping pills. The shock from the death of beauty proved numb with the countless improvements to civil rights and the constant threats from lands that once seemed fairy tale. James Meredith finds himself an education while the Navy Seals are conceived. Jack tells the world that man will be taking a small step on new grounds before the decade is finished. All of this, and Wallace is reading a paper that states,* Norma Jean Mortenson es Encontrado Muerto. *Seven years after*

1962, Wallace's vehicle is found pushed off the highway and squeezed between the scenery of the chief drainage system. Not as fit for Flannery O'Connor, but maybe, in its own dramatic way—preferably comic— perfect for the only man who understood the accent of South Louisiana.

* * *

MARCH 25, 1959.

His car came to a complete stop, caught between New Orleans and a future that had arms as wide as the river itself. The day had only just begun, and all doubt and fear were invisible and vacant. He thought of taking a turn to the Back Bay of Biloxi, but instead, turned his steering wheel in the opposite direction, off the side of the road, facing the Mississippi. His eyes focused on his future, the amount of work he wanted to return for his country. The curious road he had only then embarked upon was a stranger and one he would come to know well.

He leaned against the thick trunk of the spruce and breathed in the thin air while gazing at the deep water of the Mississippi. There were birds, of course, dodging into the blue and back up again. The sound of the rushing water carried life and reason to use time as a never-ending source. It was spring, and it showed in the newborn grass while it complemented the scenery with its color. The slight breeze ran through the worn holes of his denim, and like most who drift into the Mississippi river, Wallace felt amity and promise.

* * *

OCTOBER 1961. SAN JUAN, PUERTO RICO.

The rain fell with a slant, striking the right side of Wallace's decorated uniform. He watched from a distance as the Spanish recruits unloaded the last of their survival traits. It was the start of a new training session involving more recruits than in previous sessions. There wasn't a man involved who was looking forward to the next two weeks, but it was Wallace who had the shortest stick.

It wasn't the quick rise to sergeant or the respected work buttoned across his chest; Wallace's mind stayed fixed on the newly acquired typewriter given to him by an army buddy who had similar ambitions in life. There had been a loss of mental strength during the later hours spent alone in his office, but with an opportunity to create company, a solitary state became an option. Of average height, and a very round face, Wallace would begin to type on the typewriter every night. As though playing a piano, every tap of a key brought music to his ears.

*   *   *

Staff Sergeant Andrew Lagaeski stood over the Spanish recruits, inspecting each tag number and colored collar that came with the uniform.

"Sergeant Wallace." Lagaeski spoke over his shoulder towards the filled-out and upright man. "How soon will these men be speaking English?"

Wallace gave a curious look, and before coming to any decision, a character was born into a colorful world that had always existed, but was never expressed in such comic realism. A character he had been working on when alone over the typewriter came to life. It could have been the severe heat of Puerto Rico that finally laced between the seams of his mind. It may have been the stress of conscription, the never-ending line of recruits unable to communicate with the ones giving orders. Or, it was a secluded skill to see the obvious in the not-so-obvious that only now decided to be unmasked. Whatever time was put together to come to this vibrant scene, it put together the birth of a new man that would find himself above—and below—enlightenment.

"Well," Wallace's jaw moved circular and uneven. "That will entirely depend on their competence to grasp the excellent sounds we have put together to call the English language."

"What was that?" Sergeant Lagaeski asked in a confused and most irritated manner.

"They will be ready to take orders in two weeks, sir," Wallace corrected himself.

DECEMBER 1961.

Dear Mother,

It is difficult to know when the holiday season arrives here, in San Juan, as the weather never changes, and the skies always look the same. There is very little to no mention of the time of year. I am the only one on base fluent in both spoken languages to keep communication with the new recruits and those in command, so there is no talk of the holidays. I assure you, it is for the best. I have a curious feeling that it is done on purpose.

I must also inform you that I am embarking on my masterpiece. I have become so immersed in the character that I find that it is conflicting with my time here at base. I do believe that it will be viewed with great consideration when I leave this instrument of carnage. First, I must always remember where it is I stand, appropriate or not. I cannot and will not let this go to the hounds. I have held it in my analytical mind for some time now, but only here have I discovered the ability to put together the scenery, the personalities and the conflicts dealt in the heart of the city. Ironic, isn't it? Only when I am away from the city can I see it for what it truly is—maybe an homage to early

Twain—that is what I see in this, thus far. My masterpiece, you will understand soon enough.

After my constant studying had been interrupted, I felt no connection in reuniting with the skills I once was thought to have. I know now that was a mistake. Now that I have been given an office and typewriter, the rest is silence and due time.

P.S. I must thank you for the gift, although I am not sure how a green hunting cap will come in handy in San Juan. Maybe I will find a more personal use for the dirty thing.

Wallace thought for a moment before putting the address on the envelope. He thought about the reaction(s) his mother would gather after reading a righteous, yet riotous interpretation of a plea for attention. *I should take that word out,* he thought while knowing all along he wouldn't dismember a sentence. It was more of a description of the man inside than it was anything else. Wallace wrote the address in the upper left-hand corner and decided never to think of it again.

JUNE 1962.

Some things had changed rapidly for Wallace since October, and there was no way to avoid the changes. The last months had held countless opportunities to destroy Wallace's reputation at base. Particular barracks had been involved in behavior more suitable on campus grounds among younger generations while accusations of stolen property circulated. All the immaturity and carelessness involved Wallace to some degree. The noise brought in by the late hours had been delaying his sleep and keeping him from concentration, which stopped his development in what he considered his showpiece and true purpose for being drafted.

For Wallace, it was easy to see that the noise during such late hours had to be stopped. Being not in the situation to control it himself, he brought the issue to Staff Sergeant Lagaeski who then brought it to the sergeant first class, who then brought it to the command sergeant major. And before anything could be done about the noise, the voice reciprocated. The noise no longer suggested a celebration of any kind, but an aggressive chant against the ones trying to keep order. The source of the complement was never a mystery. Every recruit knew Wallace's tendencies to obey the rules, keep to himself and never step out of line and into focus. This, however, never bothered him as he sat in front of his green typewriter. When thinking clearly, the only thing on Wallace's mind was his work towards his craft. Little did he know at the time the noise was only the start of the revolt. Something unseen was starting to blossom, and once in bloom, there would be no way of returning to the comfortable position Wallace had found himself in upon arrival.

* * *

A black and white television sat in one deserted corner of Wallace's office. Rarely was it ever turned on—but on occasion, he would scan the three Spanish channels and catch a midnight movie, often a film he had already seen during the first screenings with his mother back home in New Orleans. *There Is No Business Like Show Business* had often played the midnight showing, which was the only reason for Wallace to pay attention to that deserted corner. Always shouting the lines, "Anne, grab your gun!" and "Midnight train to Alabama," at the appropriate times, it was a constant reminder of a time when he still enjoyed life's simpler things. And maybe that is why, as he had always known, he would fill with contempt and peace whenever the showing repeated. During times spent overseas, during the crippling pressure, the heat and the new agenda produced by those he taught English, he would often remember the lyrical, tranquil sounds of Marilyn Monroe humming the title track, and all the tension he felt would slide away. Once again, he was sitting with his mother in the dim arena with a hundred strangers' whispers. He was a child again, and there wasn't a tragedy tremendous enough to destroy the innocents. When Marilyn Monroe started to sing, nothing else would be happening.

*   *   *

"I must report a…"

"Not again, Sergeant Wallace." Lagaeski looked up from his desk with irritation. "Is this another one of your concerns about the noise? Because there is nothing we can…"

"No…" Wallace interrupted with concern. "I assure you, my situation has become much worse than the racket I endure each night." He started to twiddle all ten of his fingers in front of his chest in his nervous state, keeping close to the open door of Lagaeski's office. "It is my grandmother's ring. I woke up this morning to find that it had gone missing. Stolen! Right from under my nose while I was peacefully sleeping. That is, one of the few times I have been able to find the peace to sleep."

Lagaeski blankly stared; his jaw clocked open enough to breathe disbelief. "And what is it you would like us, here, to do about this?"

"Well, I am glad you asked," Wallace stated, pleased. "I demand a personal search party fill every room. I would like a search party that will not rest until it is found. Thank you." Wallace pulled the seat out in front of the staff sergeant's desk and took a seat with his hands folded neatly in his lap. "I will wait right here. Let me know when this horrible ordeal that has overcome me comes to its inevitable end."

"Are you joking?" Lagaeski asked. "Listen, I am not sure what is going on…" Lagaeski tapped his forehead, "…up here…but you are going to have to put this in context. You have changed, Sergeant. Your mannerisms have altered in a queer way. I cannot put a finger on it, but when you first arrived in San, you were promising. You still have potential, but it seems that your personal problems are getting in the way." He took in a long breath. "Listen, go get some rest, and come back in three days. And when you do, drop this new act you have adopted—Lord knows where it came from."

Wallace sat up in bare confusion, and for a moment, forgot about his grandmother's ring. He took in a small stream of oxygen and relaxed back into the arms of the chair. He knew the ridiculousness of what he had requested but thought it reasonable due to his title. There were words he chose not to say, and emotions he chose to drive away. He brought himself to comprehend the real situation, and remembered, *there is no business like show business.* From that moment onward, Wallace never spoke about the crimes committed against him; it was as useless as his title to be concerned, he thought.

FEBRUARY 1962.

Dear Mother,

I hate to alarm you, but the confidence I brought with me is slowly being eaten away by the constant discrimination against my best judgments. The staff sergeant has completely put my clear conscience down. This should come as a shock, as it did when I began to notice the injustice. I will soon be back in my natural environment. I am sure the institution misses my presence and insight. How could they ever think they could get along without me?

I suspect all is well with you, as I have heard very little. You must write more. Inform me of the atrocities the city has endured. I do miss The Quarter. You must venture and inform me of the changes of the full thirteen blocks of Bourbon Street—if the vagrants haven't taken it away yet.

The commander of the Caribbean arrived for a…"visit", I believe he called it. More of an inspection than anything else. He wants to position us elsewhere, away from Puerto Rico. This will work in my favor, if he succeeds. I cannot take this heat for much longer. I can assure you that I will return a changed man from the one that left. If the generals get what it is they want from me, I will return weak and degraded. Much like father—and to that, I hope he recovers quickly.

Wallace folded the unfinished letter and tucked it under a pile of books retelling the tales by Aeschylus in Spanish, translated by one he assumed never clutched the significance of the *Oresteia*—or all of Greece, for that matter. Wallace had never read the Spanish translation, but like the endowment upon Cassandra, he knew, whether anyone believed him or not. Before reading any translation from English to Spanish, Wallace promptly denounced it as a poor, uneducated attempt of deciphering.

"He probably translated this from the English and not the original Greek," he stated to himself, fumbling the book in his hands. It was only an excuse he gave himself. An excuse to not read the book. Instead, he picked up *The Violent Bear It Away*, and said to himself, "Ms. O'Connor, I prefer to visit you." He opened the cover of the novel and read out loud, "Copyright, Milledgeville, Georgia."

MAY 1962.

Wallace rushed to his office, trying to hide suspicion from any onlookers. He shut and locked the door behind him, escaping any questions for his early absence from teaching his English class to the Spanish recruits. He held in his hands a small package and an envelope he hoped would be a stable excuse to return back home. *This must be it. She must have gotten my letters hearing of the abuse that goes on,* he thought. He pulled out a small envelope cutter and carefully moved it across one edge.

My dear Wallace,

I have been receiving your letters, and I apologize for not respond-ing sooner. Your father has been ill, and I assure you, it has been taking all of my time fixing him to live proper. The thought of him living on his own, in a home, is enough to bring me to complete exhaustion. You should hear him nagging all the time about swallowing the medica-tion we get at the pharmacy. I would feel just awful for the poor nurse responsible for him.

I hear that you are writing again? The students at the institute would be pleased, I am sure. Have you kept in touch with any of them? I still receive letters to the house asking about your health. It has been months, and I still get them every week.

I am sorry about the hunting cap. I have sent with this letter a replacement. Write back soon. I would like to hear more about how the classes differ from the ones you held here.

Wallace put the letter down on his desk and glared into the opened envelope to ensure he had not missed a second paper. *How could she not mention the abuse?* he thought. *She doesn't care any more than the scoundrels I teach.*

He took the small blade he had used to open the envelope and cut the small brown box down the middle. An outstandingly lost face was painted upon him as he pulled out a long wool scarf.

Dear Mother,

Why are you sending me such outrageous attire? I suggest you learn some geography and find where Puerto Rico sits on a world map.

APRIL 1962

Wallace found the bottle of aspirin open, empty in the hands of Lagaeski, his eyes forced shut. There was a broken coffee mug on the floor that led Wallace to believe it was dropped moments before Lagaeski met the same fate. It was easy to see that the room had been in silence for some time before Wallace entered. No one had come through his office all morning, and the air had already started to smell of tired cups of coffee and the last remaining smell of burned tobacco from what Wallace had suspected was a last cigarette. It appeared to be a random act, and not a well-thought-out execution. Maybe something thought up during the morning hours, and not something that kept Lagaeski up all night. It was spur of the moment, with little to no thought— the way a man can kill another man during times of war without ever having to think of the morality behind it. It may have been during the time of day, but it seemed to Wallace that Lagaeski fired onto the wrong side.

Wallace, being well equipped in such situations, searched for a pulse, and when he found one he leaned Lagaeski up against his own desk, knowing, unlike the films, that CPR would do nothing for the situation. Wallace was not too late, as he noticed Lagaeski taking in small but difficult breaths from his drooling mouth.

That particular morning, the heat the usual day brought had procrastinated in its duty to irritate Wallace, and in its place was a cool breeze never previously experienced. On that particular morning, the church bells from three blocks away rocked back and forth initiating the new day. When Wallace had awoken on that particular morning, he remembered where he had placed his grandmother's ring: in between the pages of Homer's *Odyssey* to keep him from losing his spot. It really was all Helen's fault. The start of the day had given the impression of a promising full twenty-four hours. But in the span of two hours, with what sat between a portrait of John F. Kennedy and Wallace's full uniform, was the potential not only to destroy the rest of the day, but the rest of his career as a sergeant and a professor of English.

Wallace sat in the chair he had pulled away from the desk and thought about the consequences of reporting the incident. If Wallace were to send a report, Staff Sergeant Lagaeski would be reprimanded of his duties, be court martialed for an attempt and forever have to live with contempt and humiliation. Wallace thought about the worst ending and the finest ending possible. There was no way out; something had to be done, but what? And how? He couldn't think of an immediate reaction that would change the scenario.

When he awakes, we will forever have this between us, Wallace thought. *Maybe one day he will thank me for saving his life, and in our old age, we will sip scotch and speak about our days in the army.* He thought about his future and how Lagaeski would never forgive his actions if he were to be reported. *He would assign me the most difficult tasks on base. He could very well destroy my name and ruin me forever, or even worse, speak to the universities, lie after lie. The students back home would become much like the students at base, constantly trying to ruin me.*

Wallace stood from the chair and started to pace the room, searching the farthest parts of his mind for what he could do in which the two of them would be able to walk out of the situation without consequence. He looked toward the round clock Lagaeski had above J.F.K and noticed the amount of time that had slipped past unnoticed. He looked down at the numb sergeant, the ball of uncooked dough, and noticed faded color around his cheeks and the darkening color around his eyes behind the glasses Wallace had only then noticed Lagaeski wore.

Wallace bent a knee again to check for a pulse, only this time to find that there was nothing to find. More than just a man had been put to rest. An option too went with the sergeant. There was no man left for Wallace to save, which left him with only one option—taking one pressure off his back and replacing it with another. *What am I going to say to the sergeant major?* He knew he had no choice but to tell the absolute truth, nothing added or taken away.

Will they see this as my fault for waiting so long? He thought of all the paperwork, all the explaining, and the looks he would receive in every class when the rest of the recruits found out the story of how he took his time. *No one will understand the reasons I had to procrastinate.* There was no easy way to go about this, but he also knew there was nothing he could do from the moment he walked onto the scene.

Wallace picked up the phone, which sat on the desk of the sergeant who had relieved himself of his duties, and called for the next in command. *How am I going to word what has just transpired? How am I ever going to pick myself back up after the horrible rumors have spread around the barracks?* In his nervous state, he thought only of what was to become of himself.

He picked up the phone and glanced over Lagaeski's desk, finding a handwritten note he reviewed in his head.

I was looking for freedom, and only now have I found hope.

August 5, 1962.

Dear Mother,

It is all over. I have read of the tragedies back home. She was too young, and now all of it is gone with her. All of it. It will be difficult to watch her films now. And here I am, stuck overseas. If only I were there. How can one question their own mortality when we are constantly reminded of everyone else's? We believe it cannot happen to us because it only ever happens to everyone else, and never us. We will never die if we continue to know that others still do.

It is more personal than anything else. I could hardly believe the papers; I was questioning my fluency in the language. There is not much left to love in this world, and it seems that with each passing day, there is just a little less. It feels like it could have been yesterday you and I were entertained by Bus Stop, hoping that it wouldn't end in calamity. No one's life ends in the same manner as the movies. The world wouldn't let it happen. Our stories have been written with a more sinister pen. I believe it can be proven that God is a fan of the tragedy.

It is a shame that she will never know of the affection I had towards her and the work she produced. Maybe in another life, one not so cruel. She can rest in peace now.

I should be home soon. I do not suspect I will last much longer under these unbearable conditions. Since the death of Lagaeski, the higher-ups have wanted to retire my position as sergeant. The rest of the recruits lost all the respect I had been given at my time of arrival. Their agenda is to completely ruin my reputation, and they are succeeding at a faster rate than I had originally expected. There have been untrue stories about my involvement in the incident saying that I am to be held responsible for his unexpected passing. Where such barbarity originates, I will never know. But it won't be long before the commander sergeant major decides to cut me from this noose tied by the nonessential turn of events. And when that finally comes to pass, expect my knocking upon the door. I suspect you have left my things in order?

And one more thing, as I am sure you have been wondering about the proceeding of what will be my master work. I have put a halt to my work, as you are now aware of my situation—I have become quite collapsed under pressure. I cannot produce under such circumstances; therefore, I will have to wait until I return home.

P.S. I have found a most wonderful use for that hunting cap you sent to me over the holidays.

PART TWO

OCTOBER 1962.

Wallace sat on the window side of a Greyhound Scenicruiser with his camouflage bag and boots sitting on the aisle-side blue plastic seat. He thought of the horror stories he heard by other travelers on similar routes and how they escaped the afterlife under lucky circumstances. His thoughts during the ride never traveled further, which made a nervous distraction from the scenery. He passed the hillsides and the first sight back at the Mississippi. He missed the way a city becomes larger with each passing mile.

The plane ride had brought him to Moisant Stock Yards, where he boarded the bus that would take him to walking distance from his mother's house in Uptown, Carrollton. It had been arranged by the military at his convenience, and not a moment was spent discussing a protracted stay in Puerto Rico to sort out the differences in the substitute professor from the skills Wallace offered. Wallace had left the base with little care to what the future held for the rest of the recruits.

The memories of the barracks had passed the moment he stepped off the bus and onto the familiar grounds where he was raised. The moist air brought on an old and new feeling of freedom not welcomed with the title of sergeant. It didn't take long for the color of New Orleans to assert itself back into his mind; the characters and the graphic novel scenery had never truly left his side. He felt he was back where he belonged.

Wallace walked up the three concrete steps and rattled his wing-tipped shoes against the side of the stucco to release any dirt he may have picked up. Before he was able to ring the bell, he heard his mother unlocking the door on the other side.

"I heard you walking up the stairs," his mother expressed with excitement. "I couldn't wait for you any longer." She waved him in with both hands ready for a hug.

"Yes, well, I wouldn't get too excited. It is only back to routine." Wallace stepped through the door, dragging the camouflage duffle bag in behind him. "I would conclude that you have kept the letters I received from the university while I spent time in that… that…I do not know what to call it anymore. I have been run dry for affronts."

"Why are you speaking to me in that manner? What is wrong with you, boy?"

"It has been a long time gone. Please, give me the time to settle back in."

Wallace strolled casually into the sitting room while asking about his father's health. He found, sitting on top a cabinet, a letter from the hospital detailing the recent events in a room change.

"Well, his health declined…"

"Never mind," he interrupted. "I see you have already sent him to a home. I assume you didn't think of my homecoming?"

"It was some time," she informed him, waving her hands through the air as a sign that she didn't want to be agitated with the ordeal. She had enough trouble with the finances it caused. The last thing she would want is her son fighting back, and ultimately, wasting the money that had already been spent.

"That is fine." Wallace stopped himself from bickering. "I will visit him on my own time. I will have him know that I had no part of it."

* * *

Wallace needed a little time to get back to the routine he had left behind when drafted. The university where he taught English had changed slightly, with warnings of upcoming alterations in the faculty. His personality seemed to alter while he was away, and he had only then realized exactly how much he had turned himself into a fictional character. His mother had not changed the way she spoke to him with an insulting authoritarianism—never meaning to control, but always finding a way to insert her presence with an autocracy impossible to follow. It wouldn't be difficult for Wallace to adjust back into the environment he was once used to, as nothing had since changed. He saw many possibilities to where the future could take him. A light shone down on every possible road. The only worry he held was the chance of an alliance of half-wits putting a delay on his achievements.

MAY 1963.

Thank you for your query below. However, how it sits, I am not able to accept. I would suggest you do a rewrite for the last two chapters and clarify the overall meaning. Your focus needs to be brought out of the background and into the foreground. There is a lot of potential, and I believe with a proper rewrite you will have something worth publishing. How it sits, it is impossible to market. Wishing you the best of luck in your endeavours, and with regrets.

* * *

Through the later hours of the afternoon to the early hours of morning, Wallace would often find himself collapsed under a pile of words that made as much sense in English as it did in any other language. His failing efforts in his work started to become the only source of attention he was receiving. It seemed, as time slipped through the possibilities, that all was doomed to be buried. Soon, Wallace became less and less enthused with continuing his projects. He never believed it to be of his own fault, but that of others who did not understand his wit, his humor, and above all, what he believed to be the true voice of the Crescent City.

I am not sure what it is you are trying to get across with this would-be debut novel—but it is not for us here at ****. There is not enough story for us to take notice. The character, though compelling, does not support a moral value or something the reader can latch on to without feeling confused. In all honesty, he is quite the repulsive antihero. I suggest a rewrite, underlining the over-all message you are trying to convey. We may accept something more developed, but until then, here is the manuscript. With our apologies, and best of luck.

NOVEMBER 28, 1963

First him, *and now this,* Wallace thought as he stood over the six-foot hole dug into the soft earth. This was the month Wallace had come to know as "the month all ambition took a rest" and with this, he began to understand his own destruction and achievements. Before the death of his father, the feelings of loss only showed through his own creations and his own mind. However, from that moment on, he found all loss inevitable, and he was in control of the timing with a fraction of what would soon be gone.

As he shared the same name as his father, when Wallace looked at the tombstone, he saw himself. He saw his own name carved in stone and the amount of time he was given before he, himself, knew it to end. But Wallace never saw a grave. He never saw what was expected. All he saw was an inevitable answer to all of life's troubled inquiries. Wallace felt a comfort knowing that, in the end, all disorder and anxiety would have to learn to rest. No matter how extensive life twists and turns, on a long enough timeline, all stories end with the same tragedy. We all silently drift into a time that no longer exists, a time that was, but no longer is. Comedies are tragedies cut short.

"Why are you not crying for your poor papa?" his mother questioned, staring down the same dark hole filled with a carved wooden box.

"I had no idea it was mandatory to shed tears at a funeral." He didn't want to answer truthfully. "Maybe I am not crying because I do not understand it."

"What is there to understand? He is dead. What is wrong with you, boy? I am convinced that someone needs to look inside that head of yours. Does someone need to look inside—" She stopped. She shook her head in disbelief. "I wish I could understand. I really do—I really do."

"Be quiet, Mother, you are being disrespectful." Wallace didn't want to argue with the chance of his father listening. "Do not forget, he is not the only one to pass away this month. So show some respect, will you?"

"I just don't understand," she said, still shaking her head.

* * *

The few months that followed the death proved to be most eventful in the calamity of Wallace's progress. A road was placed before him—a road he had no choice but to travel down, and it wouldn't come to an end until years later. The university whose faculty he belonged to had gone under drastic changes, and Wallace became less and less needed. He would receive letter after letter with advice on retelling the ending to his novel. It was beginning to seem hopeless, and as the months continued, ambition fell, and the courage he once possessed while in the army slowly started to fade inside him. He had accumulated seven rejection letters before placing the manuscript in a wooden box, another coffin, and placing it on top a shelf, never to be moved again.

* * *

JANUARY 19, 1969.

"It just wasn't my duty to continue in the Institute. Now, get off my back, woman!" Wallace stumbled his words around, waving his hands in the air.

"No, no, no. It is just that you don't care about your poor mama anymore."

"You know that is not true. Stop with those kind of words. You say things you do not know the meaning behind. You do not mean the things you go on about."

Wallace stumbled into his room and started to look for a note-book to scribble down a thought he wished to keep. He heard the racket of his mother in the background wailing cryptic words and tapping on glass to create a more dramatic scene.

"Can you not hear me in here? I am under stress you have caused me," she shouted in a changed tone. "This is why they let you go. It is because you do not care. If you just applied yourself, then maybe—"

"Not now, Mother," Wallace interrupted, still searching through his things. "I must be let alone; you must not bother me when I am in here." He picked up a pile of loose newspaper articles from under his bed and started to read through the titles. *August 5, 1962.*

"And whatever happened to your 'masterwork'?" his mother asked sarcastically, jabbing her head through the door. "I haven't heard you speak about that in years. Did you give up on that as well?"

One could see in Wallace's eyes that the sarcasm lacerated an incurable feeling of regret in his pounding chest. "Well, Mother. I will have you know a great man once said, *When a true genius appears, you can know him by this sign: that all of the dunces are in a confederacy against him.*" He put his head down so as to hide his true feelings. "Jonathan Swift said that. And that is all they have done to me: What they did to him, they are doing to me. I do not expect you to understand. You never have."

JANUARY 30, 1969

The argument he had the night before with his mother was the last time he would be exposed to insult. He didn't know where he would end up, but his goals could not become more diluted. All that could be lost would be in favor to what he had become. There was no more reason to stay at home than there was to be anywhere in the world. In this situation, all things could physically change around him, and he wouldn't notice blood spilled.

It is easy for a man in his thirties to run away from home, Wallace wrote down in a used notebook with pictures of totem poles running along the sides. *When you turn of age, the care of sending a missing persons report drops by fifty percent, and when you are reaching middle age, there is no care at all.*

He gripped the duffle bag that used to carry a respected uniform and filled it with supplies needed for an extended road trip. Nothing more unusual than a green hunting cap and a wool scarf that had remained in the duffle bag for years, collecting dust and losing its color. The objects that remain in the past, the things that never change, they stay in a place where Wallace's memory could only venture. *A place no one must worry about what is happening,* he thought. *All men who live long enough outlive all hope.*

"Where is it you think you are going?" his mother asked, looking down at the duffle bag at the door. "Are you going to leave your poor mama again?"

"Let me alone," he replied without hesitation. "I suggest you look the other way. I do not know when I will be back, but when I do return, I trust that you will make yourself effective and conclude in belittling my true calling."

"What is it you are talking about, boy? You know, half the time I don't even know what you are saying to me. Go on!" she stated with a small amount of humiliation. "Go on and leave me in this deplorable backhouse."

Wallace left out the door without a reply. He couldn't begin to see that the actions he had committed over the years put little impact on his ambitions. There was nothing to help him realize that he, himself, had played a major role in his failures.

He sat in his small vehicle and felt an instant release. Something he hadn't felt in years started to return, an evolved feeling of desire and anticipation. He was never sure why he was departing on this campaign and wasn't convinced in what he was doing would change the path he stumbled upon. But as he would often remind himself: *There is nothing I can do to make things any worse. I will either move upward or stay where I sit.* Though he had found no reason to leave, he found less reason to stay.

Maybe unknowingly, he went searching for something he had lost long ago. Something he had lost during his time spent in the military. The innocence and the beauty America once had still slept somewhere out there, in the vast, unexplored wonder— somewhere *Her* heart could still be heard, singing show tunes on a black and white screen.

FEBRUARY 11, 1969.

Milledgeville, Georgia was a well-known resting spot and the last destination of a particular Southern Gothic beauty. In another time, perhaps under better circumstances, they would have met, with intentions of greatness rushing forward their inventions. He sat by the stone that read the name "Flannery O'Connor" and immediately felt the connection he knew he would in his heart.

"If the gods were as fair as they claimed—Astraea, you see nothing from the stars you beam," Wallace said quietly to himself, running his hands through the freshly mowed lawn. "Mary, oh Mary. I should have been here before '64. They never let me in Andalusia, so here is where I must find you. I told you I would visit."

Wallace started to tell her war stories, and he exaggerated the heat as the true enemy. He told the story of how he had found Sergeant Lagaeski full of pills, and why he wasn't at fault for his passing. There had been so many things, which seemed inconsequential at the time, that had ultimately given birth to the very day Wallace sat at the stone of O'Connor.

"I am not sure what happened. I am only able to remember the theater. The songs I used to sing in times of trouble. I am not sure what happened, but somewhere along the way, I became so caught up in what I thought I would become that I left who I was behind. It is true that the world doesn't work for or against anyone, and nature should never be personified. It gives false hope." Wallace stood up above the stone imprinted deep into the earth and rubbed his eyes. "In the world's timeframe, the answer for everyone becomes *not to be,*" he said, knowing that the comic still ran through him. "I guess that it was a rhetorical question." And at that moment, a character left a colorful world. A character died a short life and remained stuck in the coffin Wallace had placed on top a shelf—left with his mother. Maybe it was the cold, wet weather of Georgia, or maybe it was the stress and the shame of returning home a failure. Or, it was the realization that the world works for no one. At the end of the day, Wallace had dug one last grave beside O'Conner and buried a man he was sure kept positive company. A man who understood the Southern accent, and though fictional, truly lived in one form or another.

The stone was quite different from the stone given to his father, though, in a way he preferred it, and he was still able to see himself.

MARCH 24, ATMORE, LOUISIANA.

Since January, time had been breaking off the life that Wallace had known. The search he had embarked upon brought him to lost childhood heroes and a reason to re-evaluate his ever-reoccurring past. There was a new start since the death of the egocentric radical who believed he preceded life itself. Wallace had found that, with leaving this part of him to die, the dawn could begin, and the darkness that comes with defeat and failure would fade away. It had been almost three months since he had left home, and only now did he feel that it was suitable to re-enter the life he left ten years past. He had left no other option but to start from the beginning by erasing the latest ends. His novel would be forgotten, and he would get back to being the respected English professor he had been all those years ago. He would forget the character he thought himself to be—the character that entered his brain one rainy day in San Juan, Puerto Rico.

His car rolled into the parking lot of a dimmed tavern that had every right to be built in such a town. Wallace thought he had been driving for long enough, and he couldn't deny the obvious sounds erupting from somewhere inside him. The sun was heading in a low direction, and it wouldn't be fair of him to return home to his mother in the middle of the night after being away for so long.

He walked into the tavern and confirmed his suspicion that most of the light the building generated came from the flickering neon red "open" sign. *This is a place for the vagrants,* he thought, *but it will have to do.* He walked into the bar and pulled out a seat at the wood beside an older man dressed in black smoking leather, with patches that told stories of a rebel society.

"Good sir." Wallace nodded, in case of tension.

The man said nothing back but a grunt that left Wallace feeling a little agitated.

Wallace glanced over at the red plastic basket that sat on the counter across from the dusty man. He noticed that the bones sitting in the basket had collected grease and had been sitting there, quite possibly, since noon.

"Hit!" the crumpled man shouted at the stalky bartender who immediately followed with a 40' of the triple 'X' and splashed a splash into his short glass.

"I will take one of those as well!" Wallace shouted, sounding how an adolescent introduces himself to the kids who sat at the back of the classroom.

"Eh?" the man grunted again, glancing without twisting his neck. "It is going to drop a man like you," he warned Wallace.

"Oh, I don't think so," he replied in the same manner. "I was a sergeant in the army once. We drank this stuff for breakfast."

The man raised an eye. "Is that so?"

Wallace clasped his glass, hoping he didn't step into something he would regret in the morning. "It is, actually," he muttered, more to himself, keeping his eyes on the contents of his glass.

"Well…" The tension Wallace thought he loosened with the "good sir" vanished. "I too was in the army, ninety miles off the coast of Florida and learned to have great respect for those in command."

Wallace leaned back into his chair with great relief. "Well, you are speaking to a real gifted sergeant, here. Where was it you were stationed?"

The two spoke about the stories they experienced, and when Wallace arrived at the story of Sergeant Lagaeski, the mood dropped into the darker side of dealing with the actions overseas.

"There are always two wars being fought in those situations," the man said, stealing the conversation. "Of course, there is the war you hear about in the news, in the papers, the headlines writing the tragedies as another statistic, and then, when you are not fighting the enemy, you are fighting yourself. That is the war only you, yourself, can see and experience. It is not enough to be strong. The lack of apathy is another loaded gun we must unceasingly unleash on ourselves if you want to give the appearance of a leader." The man drank back his drink and yelled "hit", and then said to Wallace, "Sorry to say, but it sounds as though your friend lost his war. Too much emotion."

"There is no regret, I am sure." Wallace tried to lighten the mood. "He is in a better place."

"Ha! Sure he is. Underground is better than 'Nam, I guess. In a way, he did something we couldn't do—he won, as I'm sure there is freedom in *that*."

"In what? You said he lost—now he won?" Wallace asked curiously, sipping on his drink, keeping his eyes wide and focused like a child listening to a bedtime story.

The man pushed back his glass and yelled "hit". "The only way to conquer failure is to stop it in its path. Some find the only way to do that is to retreat and let everything go at once. For some, there really is no such thing as hope. It is a word we only hear others say, but the definition eludes us." He paused for a moment, and then said, "That's why I am here every night."

"And that is what happened to Sergeant Lagaeski?" Wallace asked, thinking the stranger might hold something he could use on his winding search—something Wallace could take home.

"How the hell should I know? He may have just been ill. Hit!" The bartender rushed to fill the order. "Listen, Sergeant." He turned to Wallace to see him big-eyed and curious, and he then realized that Wallace had never seen battle, and the only time he had ever seen a man die was by their own hands. "Where are you from?"

"I'm—I'm from the South…I mean, New Orleans, not too far, you know the…"

"No, no. Where are you *from?*"

"I'm—I'm sorry, I am not sure what it is you are asking."

"Well, when you do figure it out, then you will know where it is you are and where it is you are going...hit!"

* * *

When Wallace left the bar that night, he was lost in thought, wondering if the conversation he had with the crumpled man was imagined. He was looking forward to a long drive back to New Orleans, while at the same time thinking about the consequences of his actions.

He opened the glove compartment of his vehicle and pulled out the notebook he had been keeping through his conquest. *Is there more failure waiting for me on arrival? Do I want to find out?* He started to fiddle with his pen and counting the days he had been gone. *Maybe he gave me something I needed a long time ago. And what is hope? Is this the question that should have been asked by our ancient teachers? They were busy asking, "What is life?" That does not seem to be the question anymore—but is there room for hope in life? Maybe this is where I am from—and if so, I may have already reached my destiny.*

MARCH 26, 1969. BILOXI, LOUISIANA.

If I can only make it to Beach Boulevard. Up and on the darker side of the US 90, his vehicle traveling under speed, he found himself slowing down. Slowing down and slowing down. The longer it took to reach New Orleans, the more his trial was delayed. The last place he wanted to be in the world was the only place accepting him.

The long drive forced him to ponder the philosophy of the stranger he had met the night before...*hope and freedom,* the two things he had little experience with, and only then seeing clearly this fact.

His car came to a complete stop in the middle of the 90, where he sat, caught between New Orleans and his search. Continuing forward would mean accepting one fate too difficult to keep the rest of his life. He thought of taking a turn to the Back Bay of Biloxi, but instead turned his steering wheel in the opposite direction, off the side of the road, facing the Mississippi.

Of course, this wasn't what he had in mind at the start of the day, when things had a beginning and the *darkness* seemed so far away, but at the end of the day, this is where he sat. His long search seemed to have concluded without any feel to an end. His eyes fixed on the chief drainage system, but focused on something out of view.

Wallace had always understood that giving into despair was not an option, but a retreat from option, and sometimes, as he had always known, a retreat is the only direction set before one. When one gives into despair, only in the absolute end do they realize that they were on their way from the absolute beginning. Wallace could only remember a time when all things were possible, all things accessible, and it didn't seem that it had taken much time for the abyss to glare back at him. The monster he had always been fearful of, he had become.

He pulled out the notebook with the Native-artifact-printed center, and he remembered August 1962. He opened to the first page: *The only ones who ever truly give up are the ones who never had anything, in which case, what is it they are giving up? It is not giving up, it is simply accepting.*

For a moment, he remembered the time he spent in the barracks teaching English to the Spanish recruits. He remembered the first time he sat down in his office in front of the little green typewriter. He remembered the feeling of enlightenment with each finished sentence on a previously blank sheet of paper. He remembered thinking he was creating something that was worth remembering, and something that would be difficult to forget. Only now did he know what Lagaeski meant in the note he wrote, sitting on a desk in a desolate spot Wallace may have never moved from, cemented in words that he never previously thought reflected his life.

Wallace remembered *There Is No Business Like Show Business*, but it didn't have the same effect as it once did. He had forgotten how her voice had brought him closure, and he found himself forgetting the lyrics. He could only remember the title, because that was all that was left.

*   *   *

He placed the notebook on the dashboard of his dying vehicle and stepped out to breathe the thick, polluted air that rose above the green and gray river. There were birds, of course, dodging into the gray and arrowing back upward. The sound of planes flew overhead, playing alongside the sound of the river passing. It was a clouded sky, and it showed in the reflection of everything that echoed. The biting air bit the denim, and his fingertips flushed with needles. And unlike most who faintly disappear in the Mississippi River, Wallace found hope through retreat and a freedom he could give himself.

ALL THUMBS;
OR ON SECOND THOUGHT

Five. He keeps his glare upward to watch the highlighted numbers count down to his floor. His brown suitcase handle, secure in his sweaty left palm, his noticeably thin comb-over and round glasses sitting on the edge of his broad, crooked nose—this is Jordan Improve, and he has no intention of ever traveling outside the country in which he was born—which would be the United States of America. He knows calculus as if it were second nature because he was born in a home where the lawn was mowed every weekend. *Four.* Every morning, while waiting for the elevator doors to split down the middle, he focuses on the words that may or may not spill out, if one were to be inconsiderate enough to use the elevator at the precise moment he needed to ride. *Three.* If there is not another who approaches by the time the doors make an appearance, Jason is free from any form of early-morning socializing.

He looks down to the glass entrance doors of the skyscraper to see a double-breasted waistcoat with a brown leather suitcase, much like his, approach. Jason's knees buckle, his fists clasp, and the whole world becomes every step this stranger embarks upon to the socially impaired. *Two.* If Jason Improve took five minutes longer in getting out of bed that morning, this cataclysmic nightmare might have been avoided. If he had awoken five minutes earlier, just the same. *One.* The stranger in the four-piece suit stands next to him, staring up at the blinking lights in a room about to unite two people that should never be seen together. The steel doors split open, and the two walk in together as if it were a casual situation, almost as if it happened every day. The man in the suit stands next to the panel of numbered and lettered buttons starting at 'B' and ending at '39'.

"Where to, boss?" the man asks while highlighting floor twenty-seven.

"I-ya-uh…" Jason replies with a nod and a "that's the one."

The steel box, though it has enough room for three thousand more pounds, is as tight as a coffin. Jason can't help but rock slightly, unnoticeably, back and forth.

The stranger looks over with his chin up. "I hear the weather is supposed to drop over the weekend. It's going to be bad out there."

Jason looks nervously at the moving lighted numbers hitting *five* and then to the double-breasted waistcoat.

"My father," Jason says, "…my father left my mother when I was only six years old, and I haven't seen him since." He stares with wide eyes at the man who gives a similar look. "I don't think he is coming back this time."

#

You are waiting to be connected.

"Eh?"

"Oh, hello…" with an improper introduction, the customer will disconnect. "…People often find themselves spending too much money on…" a dial tone interrupts.

You are waiting to be connected.

"Ello?"

"Oh, hello. Did you know that people that switch over to *Target* can save up to…" Jason pauses, expecting to go no further. "Are you still there?"

"Yeah, I am here." The sounds of crumpling foil echoes through the line.

"Oh, thank you. I thought you might have hung up because most people—when they hear that it is me…You know? You do know, right? Why I am calling you?"

And then, a dial tone. And: *You are waiting to be connected.*

In the fifties, people went door to door. In telemarketing, the advantage rests with never having to see the disappointed faces when they realize there is no company, only windowsill pests. A marketer has less than five seconds to make a sale. This is called *fishing*. If the peddler does not convince the stranger they are worth their time in less time than it takes to answer the phone, it is over. What is rarely taken into account by those who have never gone fishing is the acute interaction and awareness that has to take place for a sale to even begin. The first second matters the most, and every second after can either escalate or disintegrate the progress of the sale. The marketer must be able to read the customer without putting a face to a word. People do not say "hello" anymore; it is a waste of time. People would prefer to say "ello", "lo" or even a quick "eh"—anything that can be as fast as a record scratch. In a society where *time* means everything, the word "hello" eats up too much life. If the marketer cannot read the tone of the greeting, if the marketer pauses longer than it takes to say "eh", then it is over. If the marketer stutters or repeats a word, it is over. Even if the hesitation is unnoticeable, it is over. The unconscious mind will hang up, there will be a dial tone and the next thing the marketer will hear is: "You are waiting to be connected." If the customer on the other end of the line answers with the rare and uncommon "hello", then the fisher is off to a perfect start, because the fisher would know that the customer has too much time on their hands. If anything, they were sitting by the phone, waiting for the telemarketer to call.

#

Four plain white walls enclose the bachelor apartment in which Jason Improve resides. There hangs a print of Jean-Léon Gérôme's *Diogenes* as a reflection of his own situation. Patches of coffee are spilt on the carpet in every direction, no more than two feet apart from one another. Evidence of spilt tomato sauce and juice from purple to pink covers the room. From his actions to his words, it is no secret that Jason has to continue to change route due to him never being able to carry out an action as planned. His life has a backup plan that has a backup plan. Everything he does, he has to do twice—not because he wants to, but because he doesn't have a choice. Because of this, during one queer situation and a confusing conversation, when searching for a companion at a shelter for rescued dogs, he found himself with four—which was twice as many as he wanted. People say mistakes are what make us human, and in the case of Jason Improve, he was more human than the average citizen. There was not a moment of his life in which he stopped being human. In fact, if he were any more human, he wouldn't be human at all.

However, this was all about to change.

Jason pours a cup of black coffee into a stained white mug. But before moving it to its destination, a thought occurs while staring down at the stains on the floor. He knows that this mug would not make it to where it belongs with the contents inside. He knows he would have to return to the steamer and pour another cup, and that would be the one to triumph over the first. He looks towards the chocolate lab in the corner, head cocked to the side with solitary eyes.

"Yes," Jason replies to the brown eyes staring at his shaking hands. "That is just what I will do." He slides the mug full of coffee to the side, grabs another from the cabinet, and cautiously pours a second cup. "This will be the one. This is the one that will make it! Why not start with the backup plan?" he continues to inform the Lab, now tapping its tail back and forth. "From now on, everything I do will be the second thing I would have done." Plan "A" was to follow through with plan "B", and if that failed, there was always plan "A".

#

You are waiting to be connected.

"Oi!"

...Oh, hello. People often find themselves paying too much money with... "Good evening, sir," With an improper introduction, the customer will disconnect. "I am calling to inform you of the benefits *Target* has to offer. How is your current wireless connection with -- --?"

On that particular day, Jason makes more sales than he has in the previous two months combined. By replacing each original word spoken, the pauses became farther apart, the words connect as if to make a sentence coherent, and he starts to sound as though he believes in what he is saying. As it turns out, Jason's second decision has, within hours, made his life seem simple. It seems that his hands have finally developed, and he now has a full grasp on the usual day-to-day situations.

The day has ended with no surprise. And for the next few months, he continues in the same fashion, and his second decisions became second nature. He no longer has to take the time to think about what his first thought was, because his second thought comes to him before the first. Having to clarify this to any of his peers would be chaos. But knowing himself better than strangers gives him the advantage of understanding exactly what was meant by "second thought first".

"Good morning, Mr. Improve," says Ivy League top supervisor, baby blue tie with little yellow ducks. He says, "Your numbers have more than tripled over the last little while," while tapping his knuckles on the desk.

It is because they can't smell me over the phone. "We get paid on commission, sir," he replies with confidence. "I have meant to step up for some time now. I have only recently found my strategy to fish properly."

"Well, you have surpassed Thomson in the sales, meaning the end of the month bonus will more than likely be put on your pay. You can count on it."

Are you sleeping? Morning bells are ringing. Morning bells are... you are waiting to be connected... "Thank you, sir. I could use it this month."

#

There was time in between the hours of working the phones for Jason to change the outcome of every evening if every action was to be redesigned a second time. The route he would take back to his apartment would alter. He would leave either ten minutes later or ten minutes earlier, but never on time. The radio station changed to one higher decimal, and the speed traveled would always be a few miles under or a few miles over. Nothing was the same, and therefore, every outcome of the usual tragedy had altered in the opposite direction.

I don't believe I will ever stop counting in my own head. "I wonder what it is like to be one of you," Jason says to the four dogs resting around him on the floor of his bachelor apartment. *All you are made of is wagging tales and wet tongues.* "You live off nothing more than instinct. You know what to do without ever having to think, let alone think again." He stands up from the floor, then sits back down. "You do not have to waste half your life thinking on how you are going to live the next moment."

He stands back up from the floor, making his way to the cupboards to pour two cups of coffee—two steps forward, one step back, two steps forward until he makes it to the hot water pot. *This would be easier if there were instructions on how to operate handled mugs...* "And if I didn't do anything at all? What happens then? Maybe all I have left are my second thoughts. Maybe if I refrain from all thought completely..." And then an alarm goes off, and Jason guesses it is the last thing people hear before life enters the final stage. His second thoughts became his first thoughts, which means he has no second thoughts, but two sets of first thoughts.

You are waiting to be connected.

And then he stands up, and then he sits back down only to stand back up again. *Is this the first thing I would do?* He takes a step forward, tripping over his untied shoelace and landing flat on his stomach.

This is it, he thinks. *I don't even know what my second thoughts are anymore.* He stands back up—stands still. Any movement now could cause his demise. He can see the clock on the oven from where he stands, and there, he will watch minute after minute pass. Minute after minute until they add to a full hour. Hour after hour, too afraid to move at all, his dogs wandering around his feet, he holds in a yawn, his knees begin to buckle, and he realizes, standing there was his first thought. In fact, there is no other thought in his head, as he no longer knows what to think. The phone rings, the dogs bark, the sun sets and the room drowns in darkness—he continues to stand, with not a thought in his disconnected head. *Everything I do is the first thing I can, and even if it is the second time I do whatever it is, it becomes the first time I succeed.* These disorganized thoughts keep Jason still the whole night. Thought after thought runs right through him. However, because every thought is slightly different from the last, to Jason, they are all first thoughts. *There is no such thing as a second thought,* he thinks. *It doesn't matter that it is the second attempt, it is still the first time I actually follow through with...*And then the phone rings and startles him to the floor where he then realizes that his floor has more stains than he can count. *One—two—three—I work in three hours. I need to be connected in three hours.* He thinks of getting up off the floor. He thinks of crawling to the phone. He thinks about the overture from *The Marriage of Figaro*—and then he thinks about getting up off the floor once more. And within the assembly line of thought after thought, he finds the thought that brought him to his feet. *Not thinking at all—that is all I am left to do.*

#

He doesn't glance at the dial that tells him the speed of his vehicle. He doesn't notice the turns that are taken or the traffic signs. He doesn't think about consequence or outcomes of any kind. Everything that is to be done is to be done without any thought, without any kind of plan. Everything is to be placed in the hands of something unfamiliar to Jason Improve. No control—the loss of all that separates him from the four dogs in his apartment.

Instinct alone—no thought involved. They say it is mistakes that make us human—and in the case of Jason, he was becoming less and less human with every hour. With pure instinct, there can be no mistakes—if something missteps, it is nature's fault, and not Jason's.

He pulls up to his office building without realizing he has arrived or knowing the exact route he took to end at his destination. He has forgotten his suitcase at home, as the thought of bringing it to work never crossed his mind. He stumbles out of his car and continues without a pause in motion towards the heavy glass doors. Before he realizes his surroundings, he is placed at his desk with the phone in his hands, listening to a dial tone, and then a ring.

"Eh!" a voice at the other end of the line answers.

And then Jason realizes that, without a thought in his head, all communication will be lost.

"Hello?" the same voice repeats.

Jason's eyes focus on the walls of his cubical, blank and vacant.

And then a dial tone, and then the female voice, and then a ringing, and then another "ello?"

Call after call, dial tone after dial tone, not a sale is made, and not a word is spoken from the end of one line. A thought starts to develop, and with all resistance, and all efforts made to conclude such enormity, the thought swirls and stirs in his brain until it becomes thick and eventually solidified. *I should probably go home now*, he thinks. He stands up and peeks over the walls of his cubical, noticing the whole staff still connected to their headsets. He does not notice the time of day, nor does it matter. He makes his way to the staircase and walks three stories up before realizing he has gone in the wrong direction. His mind, as unused as it had been, opens and takes in enough information for him to realize he placed himself in an unfamiliar office. The strange faces do not register, and the obscure smell and the unexplored ground puts him in a panic that sends him to the nearest elevator.

His heart races with a million thoughts of unknown schemes that take hold of every corner of his mind. A million repressed thoughts sprout like undying weeds in an unkempt garden. The doors to the elevator slowly slide open, as Jason turns sideways to squeeze in before they fully come to a stop. He stands in the far-right corner, almost as if to hide, waiting an eternity for the sliding doors to shut, locking him alone, inside. The doors slowly begin to move back together, but before coming to a complete close, a hand slides in to stop the process. This hand could have been the single hand of eternal rest, as it nearly had been for Jason. Thoughts do not stop taking root, as a young girl with a blue raincoat zipped up to her bottom lip casually steps into the insufficient moving box. She keeps her eyes fixed on Jason, with a stare as blank as he wishes his mind would become.

The elevator doors shut, and there they both stand—staring at each other with eyes as wide, yet blind, as their clear fears remain boundless. Keeping her eyes on the stranger, she shuffles towards the elevator panel and presses with her thumb the ground-floor light. Jason watches the lighted numbers above the steel doors light up as they move down to the main lobby.

Five. He notices a slight shake of her left hand, though only the tips of her fingers stick out of the sleeves of her blue raincoat. She continues to fix her view in his direction. He thinks of Jean-Léon Gérôme's *Diogenes* as a reflection. Patches of coffee spilt on the carpet in every direction, no more than two feet apart from one another.

Four. He feels the constant stare burning deeper and deeper. So much pressure for blundering blather, yet neither say a word at first. Both in space. Neither alone or lost.

Three. A stutter is faintly heard falling from the lips of Jason, but nothing coherent. She keeps the wide-eyed beam, blankly, blindly and adrift. If Jason does not speak, the elevator will never come to its destination. It is over. There is nothing more he can do but use his first thoughts.

Two. *You are waiting to be connected.*

And—"I heard the weather is supposed to drop over the weekend…it is going to be bad out there," Jason says.

Her eyes shudder in absolute dismay and confusion, and after great hesitation, she skips and slips. "My mother broke her ankle seven years ago protesting the rise of social networking…" The steel doors slide open. "I wouldn't worry, she is doing fine now."

THE SONG OF EREBUS

The night had fallen, and Calle could hear the wind pass through the trees and under the park benches, and from a short distance, could hear the swings in the park cradle back and forth. He opened another bottle of hops and watched the leaves dance in the trees and the fireflies hover like a thousand insignificant suns that settled in the nameless atmosphere. He found peace as he poured down the cold, soothing poison and began to remember the days he had to take time into consideration, early nights and early mornings. Then, the only time Calle needed to remember were the times *Once Upon a Bottle* and *The Tilted Glass* opened and closed. The soul was simple—and left to the better side of human cravings. He pulled from his pack a second coat and wrapped it around himself, leaving his arms free inside. Though not a cold night, the ocean a few miles away brought in a cool dew that could not be avoided. The last few bottles of hops passed through as quickly as if they were being poured down the sink, and the little green lights that floated in midair tripled and buzzed. Calle laid back against an English walnut that had branched out and draped the male flowers and Gaelic nuts in a distressing manner. He took a pouch of tobacco along with crumpled rolling paper from his inner coat pocket. He whistled lightly while, as careful as a surgeon, he placed the dried leaves along a crease down the center of the paper. As time slipped into the night, Calle pulled out a small bottle of whiskey he would sip before shifting into an unconscious state. The night became darker, more dreamlike, as the mist thickened and sank lower to the moist grass. With each sip of whiskey, he became more and more unaware of his sur-roundings. The air wrapped around him and whispered through the branches of the glooming tree. The sounds of small noctur-nal mammals rustled the dried, dead leaves, and only after Calle decided to close his eyes, when he finally thought the night could conclude as usual, did he hear another sound approach—a sound he recognized to be more than a small rodent.

"Excuse the blood." A voice was heard, crawling from behind the tree.

"There was a fire by the water," a shaky voice echoed, slowly, with a pause between every word, "—krokodil—you know what that is?"

Calle muttered few unintelligible words to the voice that seemed to lightly crawl from the other side of the English walnut.

"It peels back the skin and reveals your bones—it reveals your bones—like sticks—branches," the stranger continued. "Rot like bark—did you know about this? It is human, you know—too human."

Calle slightly opened his eyes and turned his head around to try and see who spoke like a dying animal—but the size of the tree made it difficult to see, and because of his state of mind, he did not have the strength to stand and walk around. All that was in his range of view was the back of the stranger's left arm and shoulder. He could see that his forearm was bandaged with a large red stain bleeding through, and his hand had dark holes that looked like craters on the moon, pale and dead. Calle saw the stained grass under the stranger's elbow, and then believed that the alcohol he had consumed earlier had done its job, and he was only dream-ing—and so he thought to smoke as much tobacco as possible as not to waste any when he woke.

"How little must one care?" The stranger rustled and lit a cigarette, then said with his lips pressed around the stick, "You have a
name, don't you? I am Deus—I am. Or, at least, that is what some
call me—to be honest, I am not all that sure anymore. I have been
so many things for so long, it is hard to tell where I stand these
days. But I continue as I am—as it has been much too long."

A silence fell, and all that could be heard was the stranger
sparking fire from the lighter he had been fidgeting with. A constant flash of light shot in the corner of Calle's right eye. And
then the sound of waves from the distant ocean could be heard
crashing to shore, and the smell of the grass and trees filled the air,
the stars filled the dark dome above him, and the small mammals
returned to their scavenging. Calle put his hand to his chest and
counted the beats of his heart and wondered how different he was
from the stranger.

And then, to test his dream, if it were to be, Calle asked the
only question that entered his mind while succumbing to an
intoxication that would put the average animal to sleep.

"Why are you here?" he asked. "I wish to be alone," Calle
continued. "I come here when the day is finished, nothing more.
Please." His voice rattled from his stomach. "I do not wish to be
bothered." He did not mind the stranger, but the state Calle found
himself in led him in no direction to process thought, and all he
wanted was to drift through the night like any other, pick up where
he always had before when the morning broke, and continue his
everyday routine.

"Why am I here?" The stranger repeated the question. "Well,
like I said, there was a fire by the water. And I can tell you this—I
am not here for the money." Planes could be heard flying overhead; all kinds of life took form and existed together in the com-
pressed area that enclosed around the tree. "I will tell you this,"
the stranger continued. "I have been bleeding for some time now,
and I am beginning to look a lot like the bark falling from these

branches." He said, "My bones are coming undone. Bit by bit, so that soon I will be nothing at all. You have taken part of this tree before."

Calle began to catch interest and be worried for the stranger's wellbeing. "Have you gone to a medic?" he asked. "I see your arm there." Calle pulled the bottle of midnight whiskey from his coat, unscrewed the top, reached his arm around the tree and held the bottle there until he felt it gripped away. "The clinic on St. Andrew's Drive should be able to fix that arm you have. From what I can see, they may take it away altogether."

The stranger took back a sharp swallow of bronzed whiskey. "I have tried," he said while having trouble keeping the alcohol down. "I have tried everything to get looked at, but they will not accept patients that have fallen as horribly as I." The stranger coughed a rusted growl—crackling and scratching, as though every bone in his throat shattered as he pushed an exhale out his chest with the force of a bursting shell exiting a double barrel.

From the sound of the cough, Calle understood that the stranger had accepted his last night and had left home, *like a dog*, to die away from anyone that may take care in his passing. The tone of the stranger's voice could be recognized as being absent of all concern. He had known this day was coming for a long time and seemed to have accepted it before it was noticeable. A long and painful suicide was expected and ignored from the start.

"There is nothing you can do," said Calle with a heavy heart. "There is nothing any of us can do. We all end up where you have found yourself." He wasn't sure how to let the stranger down, as he had never been in a situation where he needed to console a dying man.

"The whiskey is enough. I do not ask for anything more," the stranger replied in hopes of receiving no empathy. "It is not as though this means anything more than what is taking place under the sea or in the space far beyond the sight of any lens."

"There is a reason I find myself under this tree each night," Calle replied.

"And is it for any other reason than to say that you have chosen this over whatever it is that I am about to experience?"

"I can't say, and I do not believe I am supposed to know." Calle reached his arm around the tree and felt around for the plastic bottle. "If I am going to keep myself awake, I am going to need less blood running through my veins and more of this miracle."

"As I see it…" the stranger cleared his voice, "we haven't much of a choice. This, here, is where we have been since the beginning. And, the way I see it, so is everyone else—so is everyone else, right here." A laugh turned into a cough. "You know what they call a captain without a crew?"

"You sound awfully optimistic for a—well, your state—I wouldn't understand, but is there not supposed to be grieving and fear? Maybe it is the whiskey coming out—it doesn't have a face like a mother, does it?"

"A drifter. A leader with no followers is only a traveler. As I see it," the stranger repeated, "we haven't much of a choice—from the beginning."

"Alone?"

"Much of nothing. Fawkes's whimper." The stranger put his head down to look at the wounds he had suffered over the years, his skin peeled, cracked to the bones, bruised and bleeding, and he repeated, looking at himself, "This is how the world will end," and repeated, "this is how the world will end." And he found himself lost, again, confused about the situation. "When you are as gone as I am—and have been—things matter as they should."

"As close to the edge as you are, should they at all?" Calle asked. "I mean no disrespect, but is this what you would call your mission? Your life's work?"

"I wouldn't call it anything. Maybe a thought. But nothing more than a simple thought. There will be no one that notices after tonight. I have been gone for some time now. From the first time I began using, escaping the everyday-chaos, I have been forgotten. It is not easy to admit, but I have been dead for some time—from the mouth of a madman, I have been dead for some time now." The stranger took in a long, slow breath that crackled all the way in and all the way out, and said, "And I become one less worry to those who ever knew me before the addiction controlled my every action. And it should be so," he continued, "as, in the end, I will have made no difference and yet as much difference as all those kings before me."

"Whatever it is that runs through your broken veins," Calle said, "sounds as though it is running through your thoughts." He could relate, as the whiskey seemed to take more of a hold with each passing minute. "If you hold on through the night, I can walk you to the clinic," he said. "Everything will be just fine." As these words fell from his lips, he knew them not to be true, but never having been in such a situation, he found himself lost and not wanting to continue in conversation.

"Will you remember this?" the stranger asked.

"I can, yes." Calle thought for a moment. "But I too will end in the same manner. As I have suspected for some time, under this very tree. And after I, who will remember? What purpose do I have in remembering this when, in fact, it would mean as much for us to switch roles? And who is to say I will remember this after the effects of the drink flee with the sunrise?"

"I do not expect you to remember any more than a dog recalling its own birth. And if you do remember after tonight, I do not expect I will live on through any other means after you have passed."

Calle passed back the plastic bottle, but the stranger did not accept.

"That is enough for me," he said. "However," he continued, trying to push himself to one side, "I could use your help."

"Sure," Calle agreed, not knowing how he could be of help. All he knew was, if he did not go unconscious within the hour, the morning would come too soon, and he would not be able to set himself up on the corner with an empty hat and cardboard. And so, for Calle to be able to repeat another night under the tree, he needed the stranger to fall asleep—or pass to the other side completely. Both Calle and the stranger knew the situation, and both knew that there was no changing or going back to fix the illness they fell under. The only thought on Calle's mind was the following morning, while the only thought on the stranger's mind was whether there would be another morning.

The stranger began his request, "If you could reach into my pocket, you will find a syringe packaged in plastic."

Calle understood what was asked of him, and taking in consideration the state of the stranger, found there was nothing that could harm him any more than what he had already done to himself. Calle found the strength to move to the side and face the stranger for the first time. He could see his skull from where he had previously torn out his hair. Blood dripped down his face like teardrops from where he had picked away scabs. Most of the blood had dried, blackened on his torn clothes that resembled rags stitched together. His eyes had lost all color, his teeth were missing and only cracked, dried gums could be seen, as his lips had been peeled back. His age was not clear, but it was easy to see he had long expired, and his life had passed, not only through time, but through memory and lives that he too had forgotten.

* * *

Calle lay back against the tree on the opposite side of the stranger. The whiskey had been running through his veins at a steady pace, but he did not feel a separation between the way he felt at that moment and the way he would have if he had nothing to drink at all. Too much of the night had passed for him to sleep and awake in time for the morning rush hour.

"This will be all that is left," the stranger mumbled low. "Anything more, and there would be a reason to continue."

"Are you afraid?" Calle asked, letting go of all hope for the approaching day.

"There is nothing there to be afraid of," he answered.

"Absence can be terror."

"Only when we are aware can absence of all things seem dark, but it cannot be terrifying if terror itself vanishes along with self. I understand this better now than before. I have experienced all that I wish to, and now it is time for those things to be forgotten, lost, as though they have never been expressed through an essence of any kind. To be what we were before this. A place where fear has no room. Khaos sings while Aion listens—in the arms of Erebus, hold me still, and hear nothing more."

The sun began to rise as the sky turned to gold, and the birds in the trees made a soft and lucid sound.

"I have forgotten your name," Calle said, hoping he would be able to remember.

"So have I," replied the stranger. "There is no more need for me to remember. It has been a long day," he repeated. "It has been too long of a day. I think I will sleep now." A silence fell as he took one last look at the sky. He shook is head in anger and said, "I thirst. I thirst. And it never began. This too is out of your hands." The stranger closed his eyes as his chin fell to his chest.

A cool wind blew through the tree, and Calle then knew he was alone. He thought about the fire that was mentioned by the water. He thought about how much whiskey was left in the bottle, and how it would serve him for the first few hours of morning. With all that was left, he thought about how much tobacco lay resting at the bottom of his pouch.

And when the sun burns out, and all life fades into space, if a voice could be whispered from that glaring abyss, it could say, "Nothing ever happened here." And it would be right.

FIFTY THREE

From the start, Fifty Three will follow the same action every character has followed from the beginning. Fifty Three is about to come to life. Fifty Three cannot remember the last time he was brought into this world, and he will not remember leaving. To him, this is the first time he has ever come into existence. To the character that is Fifty Three, life is still unknown until these words continue off the page, breathing life into the impossible. When this ends, so will Fifty Three, and everything will find itself in full circle. There are places in the universe that exist due to belief.

#

This world has zero dimensions.

"Hello?"

"Not now, Fifty Three." For the moment, Fifty Three does not speak. He does not know a word of English. Not yet. But he will understand this: I am setting a world in which Fifty Three will be placed. *This* world has zero dimensions, and yet, it can exist in any form imaginable, and only if imagined.

Fifty Three is about to learn how to speak English.

"What?" Fifty Three asks. "What is going on? Who is this? And who are you talking to? Where am I? How did I get here? And more importantly, where was I a moment ago?"

To some, this is more than reality, and it is the only way to understand life.

"Settle down, son," I tell him. "You are just a character of a story I am currently creating. There is very little you know about yourself at this point in time. I haven't even thought of a proper name for you, let alone a history or personality. Hell, I may not even use you. I may have to toss you out with Sally Wayloft and Jane Marilyn. They didn't work well with this."

Fifty Three starts to realize what I mean by "toss out".

"What? How can you say that? You have already brought me in. You can't get rid of me like that. Can you?" he asks. "Who left you in charge? And you have given me a name; I heard you say it."

"Your name is Fifty Three for a good reason."

"Okay, okay. So, give me a past. Quick!"

"Fifty Two," I tell him. "And your future is held in Fifty Four."

"Okay. That makes sense. Now, at this moment, what is it that I do?" Fifty Three asks. "What? Why did you say, 'Fifty Three asks'?" Fifty Three asks. "Stop it! I know what I asked."

Fifty Three does not know that there is a third party involved. But he is figuring it out quickly.

"I am letting the reader know," I tell him. "If I do not tell them, they may think it was me asking, when it was really you, Fifty Three."

"The reader?" he asks. "Who is the reader?"

"It is whoever is reading this at any given moment," I tell him, and make sure he understands. "Go on, you can say 'hi'."

"Hello, reader," Fifty Three says to you. "Okay. I think I am beginning to understand. Or are you only writing down that I understand, when really I have no clue?"

Fifty Three is catching on to the process.

"Well, that is up to me. You see, Fifty Three, I have to put you in a situation you may or may not like. You see, I may have to put you through painful scenarios that have no good outcome whatsoever. Or, I could trap you on an island full of everything wonderful. It really depends on what mood I am in."

"And what kind of mood are you in right now?" Fifty Three asks.

"I am not sure," I reply. "I was bored, with nothing to do, so I thought I would bring you into the picture." Fifty Three understands fully, and I tell him, "If I get too bored I may set you on fire, throw you in batter and serve you for breakfast to the lost monsters in the forgotten stories under my bed."

Fifty Three starts to feel helpless.

"But what if I don't want to be breakfast? Is there anything I can do to stop you from throwing me in a fire?" He starts to panic, and he says, "Stop this now!" Fifty Three becomes so overworked his heart races frantically. He really does believe I am going to throw him into a fire, though I have no intention of doing so. He then says, "Is that true?" He quickly brings himself to calm down. "So, you are not going to throw me into a fire and feed me to whatever is living under your bed?"

"No," I reply. "I have something much more interesting for you. Instead, I am going to send you into the future."

"The future?"

"Yes. With semi-cosmic rays, the abhorrent first-class feeding off machines, skies full of dark smoke from a steam-punk fantasy, you will be able to see things I can only imagine."

A room becomes full of neon lights and radioactive sunlight. The sound of innovated mechanics buzz and calculate every possible outcome of Fifty Three's actions. The whole room is wrapped in tinfoil, switches that turn on the apocalypse, and strobe lights that twirl in unison. Fifty Three understands his situation and immediately starts to reminisce of his younger days when he drifted down the Saint Lawrence with his Labrador, Jasper.

"Those were the better days," Fifty Three says. "A time when I wasn't surrounded by these inventions that were designed to make life easier." He says to himself, "It has all failed."

Fifty Three begins to comprehend this sentence as it is being read, and he realizes that he doesn't have to be feeling the feelings that he is feeling.

"Do you understand now?" I ask, knowing that he understands the situation.

"So, could you make me a bionic man so I have no memories of Jasper?"

"I could, yes," I tell him, "but it is not that kind of story."

"What puts me apart from a mechanical person if I have no power I control? If my will is by your command…" Fifty Three starts to move his hands into the pockets of his blue jeans. "Wait! What am I doing?" He pulls out a thin silver needle. "What am I doing? This isn't what I want to be doing. Not at all." He holds out his index finger, lightly stabs himself, and watches a bubble of blood enlarge. "Ow!" He smears the blood on his torn jeans. "Why would you make me do such a thing?"

"If you were a machine, you wouldn't bleed," I tell him. "If you can't bleed, I have no use for you."

"You are an evil god," he says. "What then do you have planned? Are you just going to throw me around until you get bored of me and kill me off?"

"As it has happened before, and will happen again."

"What is meant by that?"

"Well, it is not entirely up to me. There is a third party involved."

"The reader?" Fifty Three asks—knowing all along. "What is it the reader does to keep me here?"

"Well, believe it or not, this has happened many times before. This exact scenario has played out every time someone decides to read these pages."

"Pages?"

"Never mind," I tell him. "I am going to have to develop this immediately to give a sense of motion."

"What do you mean? Is this not how this works?"

"Not at all. For the third party, this is becoming tedious and predictable."

Fifty Three starts to feel a shift in the atmosphere while his two-dimensional world becomes more chaotic, more real and self-involved.

"What is going on? What is all of this?"

"The world has to change for you to exist. For you to exist, there must be a climax and there has to be a tragedy."

"A what? What is a…whatcha call it?" Fifty three asks while keeping balance on the shifting floors. "Can't I be left alone? Can't you just tell me what I am about to do?"

Fifty Three starts to run along thin blue lines as the scenery starts to paint around him. Shapes shift and decline down a two-dimensional canvas. Fifty Three slides and transfers into another dimension, one more resembling a cube, four corners and a distance. A bending sphere of compact matter flies over his head, breaking into thousands of pieces and shaping into thousands of black birds. This world has never been so immense and alive.

"What is going on?" Fifty Three asks as he meticulously averts and dodges the kamikaze black birds with their salient beaks aimed towards his dancing feet. "Stop this! Stop this now!" his nervous voice squeals. "You are going to hurt me, and for no good reason." The black birds come to a halt, and the noise burns out. Fifty Three stands silently in his torn, tight blue jeans, thinks, and says, "You made me say that! You made me say 'for no good reason,' which means—you know. The very fact that I am speaking any of these words I am speaking shows that you already know this is all being done for no good reason."

"This is true. I do know," I tell him.

The black birds reunite back into a colorless sphere over his head. The sphere then moves into the distance and starts to burn in saffron. Carolina blue starts to invade the edges of the sun, and it moves outward until it conquers itself a fully bloomed sky. Fifty

Three has never felt so harmonious and separate from the despair he once felt from the loss of his partner.

"Is this true?" Fifty Three asks. "There was a time I wasn't alone?"

"A time, yes."

"Then why do I not remember it?"

"You will in *three...*" I first must think of an accident. "*Two...*" Fifty Three is not going to like this. "*One...*"

Fifty Three breaks down and starts to weep uncontrollably.

"She was only twenty-three years old," he yells to the circle in the sky.

Her name was Thirty Seven, but eventually everyone would call her Eternally Vulnerable. Even though nothing was her fault.

"I see what you did there," Fifty Three says.

She was left-handed. This means she would only read left-handed books. This means, while she was being taught in school, other children would dance around her. "Everything she does is upside down," the other children would say.

"Poor Thirty Seven." Fifty Three shakes his head. "We were going to get married on a hill. She was going to take my last name, Three. She was going to be Thirty Three."

"But none of this happened," I tell him. "Because when she was only twenty-three, she accidently pulled a right-handed trigger on a left-handed gun."

After Thirty Seven brought death into Fifty Three's world, things were never the same.

"She was completely obscure and perplexed at the time," Fifty Three tries to explain. "It should have never happened. Not in that way."

But it did. It had to have happened the way that it did.

"But you also have to understand," I tell Fifty Three, "it is not entirely my fault."

"Surely you are not suggesting that I..."

"No, no, no. It is the third party, the reader. Because the reader has continued in this nonsense, it had to happen."

"And if the reader had stopped only moments before?" Fifty Three asks.

"Then her existence would have never come into play."

What Fifty Three has failed to realize (until this sentence comes to an end) is that the only two reasons this has come to pass is because I have decided to write it, and because you, the reader, has decided to continue to breathe life into the story.

"This means I could be happy if you wanted me to be." Fifty Three forgets about Thirty Seven and says, "It is not my choice at all. None of this is. You have already written this all down, and I am only playing it out. This is your will, not mine. Is it possible for me to have a say in what I say? The fact that I am questioning this at all doesn't make much sense, unless…" Fifty Three ponders the relevance of finishing his sentence.

"That is correct," I tell him. "But you have to remember that this will all end very soon."

"And then what happens?" he asks.

"Do you remember what it was like before the reader started reading this?"

"No."

"Well, that is what it will be when the reader is finished." I tell him, "Unfortunately, there is no way in which I can explain this to you that you will understand."

"Does this mean I am going to die?" Tears form at the edge of Fifty Three's eyes.

"In a way, you will die, eventually."

"What do you mean?"

"I mean, at this moment, you only exist inside the reader's imagination," I tell him. "I put you there. I invented you, Fifty Three, to float around in someone else's head."

"So, when they are finished reading, I will no longer exist?" His heart starts to race, and he says, "But I don't want this to end."

"Well, in a way, it doesn't have to," I tell him as he starts to realize that there could be a pleasant conclusion to all of this. Something with hope. "You see, Fifty Three, you could very well live forever."

"But eventually the reader will come to an end, which will terminate me."

"Not exactly. You see, there is a place you can go in which you can live forever."

"Is it a nice place?" Fifty Three starts to experience a unique perception of his own reality.

"You have to understand," I tell him. "You now exist in the reader's mind, and you will continue to exist there long after they are done reading about you. You will live on through their memory, which in a way, is how you exist now. Only when all is forgotten, will you cease to exist."

This seems to comfort him.

"So, will they remember me?" Fifty Three asks.

"For now, all you can do is believe that they will. Everything else has already been done."

The circle pasted against the blue sky starts to fade back into the colorless form it once was, and as if it were never there, it falls out of Fifty Three's world. The color in the background starts to eat itself up until it is nothing but a pinpoint in Fifty Three's left eye.

"What is going on?" he asks. "What is happening around me?"

"Your story is coming to an end."

"Am I scared?"

"Maybe a little. But I will make sure you do not mind."

The little bit left of Fifty Three's world starts to fade away, but he doesn't mind it too much. He knows it is not quite the end. All color lightens but the blue in his torn, tight, short-ended jeans. He shuts his eyes and remembers the first time he tried Italian food.

"Is this where I say goodbye?" he asks. "Before it is too late?"

His legs and his arms start to dissolve away as he becomes more and more like his own memories. Colorless and shapeless, like the space between these lines, it all evaporates. All that remains is the memory, if you wish.

And just like that, Fifty Three is put away with *stellar* and *the rest* until another third party initiates his life again.

FLECK

The news channel had been on the screen of every television around the world for the last thirteen hours. There were no intermissions, no advertisements, no other channels with reception. Families had grouped together, holding hands and holding their breath. No one knew what this meant. Forty-eight hours ago, nothing seemed out of the ordinary. The world spun in orbit and looked as though it would continue as before without interruption. No one could have predicted what was to follow. No one could see what was about to take place, as it was something that did not enter anyone's mind previously. From the United States to Japan, and every country in between, every family with a television watched, and those with only a radio listened. The whole world was held silent, every mind awake and alert to what was being broadcast. A countdown had begun, and there was nothing anyone could do to stop it from continuing. Twenty-four hours earlier, everyone on the small planet had plans for their life, their future, and thought they knew what was to happen the following day. But everything had changed when they turned on the television or the car radio. One by one, they all tuned in to listen or watch the countdown. Though they were not directly told what it meant, everyone, in unison, knew. A sense fell over the world, and everyone knew, when the seconds pulled back to zero, time would cease. No one knew exactly what it meant, but everyone felt the same notion, a sense of urgency, a feeling of helplessness. It was as though something had been placed in the minds and hearts of every living thing, and they had all, in unison, decided that this was the moment something larger than themselves would make itself known to every conscious mind in every conscious country. Not a soul was sleeping; everyone was fully aware of what was about to take place, and they listened onward. Somehow, without any reassurance, it had quickly become stamped in every heart, and etched in every mind that when the countdown finished, time would be made away with. Those that strayed into the street felt no need to riot, no need to cause any commotion.

Some held still with a rosary dangling from their closed fist, eyes wide and fixed. Many were gathered around a bar, watching a single television hung in a dusty corner. Some sat in their garage with the radio on. Those that did not have access to television or a radio looked to the sky, sensing a change. Every god was given prayers; many beliefs were abandoned. No one had prepared and no one knew how to get ready, as it never occurred to them before that such an event would ever transpire. Everyone held their breath and waited as the end of the last hour approached closer and closer.

The people in the bars, and the few on the streets, had their small conversations about what would happen when time ceased to exist. It was difficult for anyone to understand the future or the past, or understand the meaning of the situation in the context of political affairs, family affairs, humanity's natural instinct to want to move forward as a species. Suddenly, within the last hour, everything the past held seemed to be vague, unimportant and outwardly absurd. Continuing a future after the last hour seemed to have already been placed with the past. The complete works of Shakespeare, Apollo 11, every revolution and the fall of Gorbachev's wall seemed to dissipate—a renewal or a complete dismissal of everything past and present.

Messages from world leaders appeared randomly throughout the countdown. *My fellow citizens, I stand before you in the midst of a crisis*—the timer, placed in the right-hand corner of the screen—*Though the threat is unrecognized, it is clearly understood, and soon we will be facing a new era. We no longer unite under one nation, but are contrived to unite as one life—we are no longer countries divided*—what was to be expected, and nothing more. Few took notice of the speeches, watching the dead eyes of the speaker, and thinking all along about the wasted time and if it meant anything if the time was spent on anything else. *Let it be told to the future world that in the depth of winter, when nothing but hope and virtue could survive...that the city and the country, alarmed at one common danger, came forth to meet...*The sky darkened all over the world, and a silence fell as every heartbeat thumped in accord.

The families that were together huddled closer as the time neared. The lonely ones grasped their drinks tighter and tighter, until the glass nearly collapsed in on their sweaty palms. All groups of people were united in the sense that they all shared in their honest cowardice. The news reporters fell silent, the sound waves from the radio halted, and not a rush of wind would rustle through the trees.

And in an instant, time had stopped altogether. Children glared upward at their mothers and fathers, siblings and relatives, as if all at once, every secret was reviled, nothing hidden and nothing sacred. A feeling of complete abandonment and worthlessness swept through the streets, through the taverns, through the homes and villages across the globe. The last second had happened—and after it had finished a sense of belonging in the unreserved space of improbable senselessness devoured all aspirations, all prospects and interest—along with fear and worry.

It was the end of time, but the world still spun. Time had just ended, and there was no time left to stress over the complications of life. No more time for arguing over philosophies or ideologies.

No more time for war or decisions involving order of any kind. Time had come to an end, and for the first time, the whole world truly felt alone, suspended in space. Without time, there was no use in continuing toward progress. No use in caring about the future or the past. No use in fearing the unknown or known. It was over—and the world just sat there, like an untouchable rock in an open field.

PARABLES

ON THE PATH

On the path, enveloped by forest, traveled the congregation. For the most protracted time, they moved in accord with eyes observing forward. He moved along with the circle, as he always had before. A constant eye on the unnamed, unfolding aisle.

And then a voice was heard—a prescription for freedom. And he was in the company of everyone else, on the road that releases from doubt. And when he found himself listening to what he heard off the road, he wondered if the rest heard. Of course, curiosity has never killed a creature—and such is an example of every living thing. So he listened, because beyond the path only inquiry existed. The road was clear with only certainty as they all moved forward.

But there he stayed, on the road, because there was a comfort being in the company of imitation and likeness. So he listened and listened, and interest grew, and it grew, and it went straight through him, and through him. And when the curiosity grew, the voice off the path grew—into the thick wood that enclosed the road they all traveled, there was something unfamiliar—and he knew this. He thought to get closer to the edge, to the edge of the path, and as he thought this, he noticed the congregation had moved ahead. Time had come to something less known—the voice in the thick wood had grown, the rest were in the distance—visible, but as a glimpse alone. He had thought he had felt an acceptance to travel off the path—a prescription for freedom. And there he took his first step off the path, and when glaring down to where he had once been, he knew—he heard—*this is an exemption from.*

The community could only be seen in whispers, and the voice in the wood was heard through wails of eagerness. From the side, he moved into the heavy wood, in the direction of the voice. As he moved in deeper, he observed the direction of the voice and obtained nothing. The closer he came, the more silent it grew. And the more silent it grew. And the more silent it grew, the deeper into the wood he found himself. There was no longer a direction in which the voice traveled. He searched, as repetitive, and repetitive as all the worlds before him.

The voice had finished, and there he stood. Lost in every anxiety of the unfamiliar. The path could no longer be seen, and the voice was no longer heard. The earth had grown around him, and in every sight stood an imitation of the opposite direction. He waited, still. And the longer he waited, the darker the wood became—the longer he waited, the more it flourished like the obscurity devouring the light.

And then a sound was heard. The sound of a thousand steps taken and a thousand words spoken. The congregation on the path then replaced the voice in the wood, but he could no longer reach the path he once traveled, because there it had been, and there it could never be seen again.

IT COULD ALWAYS BE WORSE

It was the start of a new day. The sun pierced through the few clouds that touched the skyscrapers, and the wind had settled along the busy streets. A displaced wanderer stood on a busy street corner in downtown New York City, wearing nothing but torn cloth and a blanket wrapped from shoulder to shoulder. When the public passed him by, he would often be asked about his choices in life, and he would only ever reply with, "It could always be worse." He stood on that street corner every day, through the rain and through the snow. He had been on that same corner for so long that the locals recognized his face, and he became a tribute to the dispossessed individuals that settled with their misfortune. To most people that passed him by, he was only an object of charity, but within himself, there was much ambition and promise.

The optimism in the distressed and the impaired is one of the incredibly surprising conditions in the human spirit. There are many people whom, determined by the typical, one would assume to see hopeless and undetermined, yet their state of having positive beliefs triumph over the average character.

After speaking with people that have crippling financial complications that have left them impoverished, they continue to hold an irrefutable positive outlook on what the future holds for them.

A wanderer stood on a busy street corner in New York City wearing nothing but torn cloth and a blanket wrapped from shoulder to shoulder. He was selling sketches of the way he saw everyday life. Before passing him, a man asked, "How does a man in your position continue to live with expectation and enthusiasm?"

Apart from his usual answer, he told other stories of other people's personal burdens and how they conquered their sorrows and afflictions, gaining values and integrity when life provided. He told me, "You cannot keep a poor man down forever."

It continued in the same fashion for some time, and after hearing these stories of perpetual happiness, most could conclude that all these people had a single thing in common, and that is that they did not foster any self-pity. It became clear that it was not hardship or ill fortune that brings the human spirit down, but mourning one's own sorrowful property. Drowning in past complications is what ultimately would bring all of these people to a state of complete despondency, and therefore it was preserved away from their belief. Suffering is a universal experience, and there is no life without it. But history is a witness to the truth that we need not be creatures of circumstances, but creators of them.

A BAR NAMED WORK

A man walks into a bar. He sits at the wood and asks for something strong, something with green, no fruit and nothing sweet. With the way time sneaks through glass after glass, the man's phone sounds its alarm. He answers to find his wife frantic with concern for his whereabouts. Having lost track of time, he can't find an excuse quick enough to lower her nerves and has no other choice but to tell her the truth.

"Where is it you have been?" the women on the other side asks with concern.

"Honey!" he replies to assure her of his safety. "There is no need to worry. I am only at *work,* and I will be home soon."

The man places his phone back into his pocket where it stays for five minutes before it, again, starts to vibrate. He takes it out and, this time cautious, views the name that appears on the blue screen. He reads the name of a co-worker and decides to suggest company.

The man looks towards the flat screens above the shelves of alcohols and says into the phone, "It is four to three, a full period left." The man calculates the time on his Bell and Rose and the amount of ice-time left above the half-empty bottles. "I am at the bar on twelfth and third, down the block from the site."

Though his stories are true to his wife and friend, the truth is more dependent on the accuracy to communicate what is being said than what is found in the integrity itself.

THE GUARD

Vir worked out his morning routines. He flossed between his teeth every morning an hour before the sun rose. He polished his shoes and chose his tie—and a moment before the sun beamed through his open window, Vir was organized and equipped for the entire day. He poured his coffee and went for his morning paper—but as he opened the front door to receive the morning news, he was greeted by a man in uniform. A guard's uniform, with shoulder pads that laced across his shoulders.

Surprised, as one would be, Vir questioned the guard, "Sir, is there something I can help you with?"

The guard did not speak. He had hardly moved at all until Vir slightly shoved him to one side to walk down his paved walkway to retrieve the rolled newspaper.

"Here," Vir stated sternly, pointing the rolled paper in front of the face of the guard. "You listen, I do not know if this is a game you intend to fool me with, but you best be leaving before I call for you to be taken away."

The guard looked him in the eyes and then began, "You are to do as I say. Anything that I tell you to do, you must follow through completely. Do you understand?"

Vir glanced from side to side, then back into the eyes of the guard. "Excuse me? This is where I live. You cannot tell me what to do!"

"I have been sent here," the guard replied. "I have been sent here to tell you what to do, and if you do not do what I say, I have every right to put my gun to your chest and a bullet through your heart. Do you understand?"

Vir looked down the side of the guard to see a dueling pistol locked in a holster. Confused, but not shaken, Vir asked, "Who sent you?"

The guard replied, "I have been sent here to give you commands; if you do not follow through with what I tell you to do, I will shoot." There was a short silence. "Now," the guard continued, "you may carry on your day as usual. You are free to do as you will."

Vir, slightly startled, backed away and shut the door behind him. He carried on through his day, waiting for the guard to give him orders. He paced back and forth throughout his own home, waiting and waiting, but never did an order come that day.

The next morning, Vir awoke and he flossed between his teeth one hour before the sun glowed through the window. He poured his coffee and went to fetch his morning paper. Upon opening his door, he noticed the guard had stayed overnight by the side of the door.

"I figured you would have left!" Vir exclaimed. "You did not give me any orders yesterday. Why are you still here?"

The guard only said, "You are free to do as you will."

With that, Vir walked down his paved walkway, grabbed his morning paper and walked back indoors. Again, he waited, and again, nothing came. He decided to leave his house for groceries, and as he did, the guard stood still.

As days turned to months, Vir grew more and more hesitant, waiting with each day for his orders from the guard. And as seasons turned and years began to show on Vir's face, the guard never moved from his post. As time moved forward, Vir quit asking the guard what he was to do, as the guard would only give the one response, "You are free to do as you will." And so he continued to do as he willed, but never once did his mind stray too far from the guard.

Vir had long grown into an age that was recognized by the seasons, and he knew he was given little time left to continue. He stepped out onto the front deck where he sat in a chair that faced the guard, who had never left his post.

"You know," Vir said, "I am now too old to be of any use to you." The guard stood silent. "I am still unsure what purpose you had in mind, why you have not yet shot me, or why you ask nothing of me—I am unsure of it all."

The guard, noticing that Vir was about to die, turned to face him and asked, "Now, did you live your life as you wanted?"

"Yes," Vir replied. "You asked nothing of me, so I lived my life as if you were never there."

"You did! Now tell me," the guard replied, "were you ever really free?"

THE FIRE

When there was a fire in his apartment building, and the starving flames ate up the walls, and the books, and the papers and the pictures of people, he only thought of how many pennies he had in a coke bottle that sat under his kitchen sink. He lit a smoke and thought it mocking the situation, and thought to himself, *It is a cold night for a fire.* The sirens arrived in their flashing American colors. An audience gathered to watch lives change as their positions turned to something unfamiliar. It was a funeral in such a sense.

And then he noticed the paper flying out the windows—all work-written material, surely some poetry and more likely studies of history. And then he thought, *Is that ironic? Burning history books? Making history that tells of history?* And then came the whispers from the audience, after the initial shock had kept them silent for so long.

"Do you live there?" a lady from the crowd innocently asked the man.

There came no reply, but his initial thought was, *Of course not, you half-mind, the place is on fire.* However, he also knew she meant "did" and not "do".

This was going to happen, he thought. *Ashes to ashes,* he thought. As the smoke reached the height where it disappeared into the night, a shout was distinguished from within the building, to which he then thought, I *guess I have it alright.*

His eyes filled with flames while his lungs filled with smoke. His reaction was silent while his mind schemed nonsense. *Live for the moment? What a stupid thing to say. As if it is possible to live at any other point in time.*

"You will need to step back," a man in a 451 helmet said to him.

"But I once lived there." He pointed up to the sixth floor. "Or, no, maybe it was there." He lowered his hand to the fifth floor. "It is difficult to tell at this point, but somewhere in that future wreckage will be everything I once owned."

The absence of all emotion and despair resonating from the man who stood to watch his assets turn to smoke puzzled the man numbered 451.

"Well...I am sorry," he brought himself to say.

Sorry? the man thought. *Did he just confess to starting the fire?*

And from there, the man put his hands in his coat pockets and strolled toward a train station that had closed down for the evening. He sat on a waiting bench and looked at his wrist, finding out that he had left his watch in his apartment. *God bless—God damn,* he thought. The night grew thick as smoke from the fire that traveled with the man. And then he thought, awaiting the morning train, of the time he spent in Alaska and Mount McKinley, and if there were any winners of the Power Ball the night before last. He held his back to the fire, where a dim light could be seen warming the city. The smell of a campfire spread for miles. There was a faint sound of water rushing—a white noise—a train so many miles away. The wind brushed the tracks and brought fallen leaves around his feet. He noticed a tear in his coat pocket as he fingered through, stretching the hole wider and wider. He then leaned, his back pressed against the cool bars of the bench. He shut his eyes and began to count, in the back of his mind, the pennies he had kept in a coke bottle under his once kitchen sink.

THE POPLAR TREE

A poplar tree stood over the luxurious house of Treadwell, who spent his time alone with his many belonging—some obtained illegally, and some thought to be of rare origins, to which kings and queens would be jealous. And though he had the diamond-encrusted eggs, the rugs that would be fit for the Taj Mahal, and the ivory tables made from endangered species, he gave more attention and praise to the poplar tree that shadowed everything he owned.

"This here," he would say. "This here was grown from nothing. If it weren't for me," he would continue, "it would not be here at all."

After a long day of admiring his tree, resting underneath the shade, or simply gazing at the yellow and white flowers that blossomed during the spring, he would find himself at his fireplace, cozy, with a glass of red, pondering what he could obtain to make his tenement appealing. Though every guest's eyes wondered in amazement as they toured his halls, Treadwell always wanted more. After a day of being in possession of a new work of art, he would grow bored, and the following day find himself searching through the local art galleries for new material.

He found himself spending more and more time with and around the poplar tree. He had purchased a mandolin and would sing songs to the leaves. He had purchased an easel, canvas and paints and would paint portrait after portrait of the branches, bark and background. It seemed that year after year, the tree would double in size until it no longer looked like a poplar at all, but something grown from magic.

After the years had gathered many belongings, Treadwell could no longer sit in his usual chair by the fire, as the fireplace had been stocked full of jewelry, and his chair was buried under canvases, plaques and little artifacts. He stood, trying to pour a glass of his favorite color, but found he had no elbow room. So, deciding to worm his way through all of his treasures, he thought it would be more fitting to be placed outside underneath the tree.

He squeezed through the door to the outside and quickly shut it, leaving him outside in peace. Treadwell walked underneath its stretched branches and tipped the bottle of wine he carried with him. He placed himself at the roots and drank until the sun started to make an appearance, and his eyes and mind began to shut.

When Treadwell finally awoke, he noticed that he had slept through the better part of the day. He rose from the ground and headed towards the door of his house. As he turned the handle, he noticed that he could not open the door due to the cluster that had been building up inside. He had locked himself outdoors with all of his belongings inside. Pushing harder and harder, he found there was no use; he would need something to slam against the door in hopes of shattering whatever was on the other side to let him back indoors.

He looked for rocks, but could find none strong enough to penetrate through. He finally looked over at the thick trunk of the poplar tree, and thought, *If there could only be a way for me to throw those roots through the door.* He paced towards the towering tree and fell against it as a tired worn man. And as he did so, he heard an eruption from the core of the wood. Treadwell backed to one side to watch the tree split up the middle and fall over onto the roof of his house, crashing through all of what he owned and destroying everything he had spent his years achieving.

Though the outside of the tree appeared healthy with green leaves and yellow and white flowers, the inside had been rotting with mites that ate away from the inside. The mites had been eating away for years and years, not being able to fill their bellies. No matter how much wood they devoured, they kept on eating until they had destroyed the very home in which they resided.

THE HAYSTACK

It was supposed to be a dry day where dead leaves found it difficult to detach themselves from their stems, falling softly to the ground around me. I can see from the clouds above me the sky will roll in the wind and sitting alone in an open field as I am is hardly where I want to be. I am not sure how it is I have gotten here or who it was that put me together, but here I am, sitting in this field, all raked up into a large pile for reasons I am unaware. A moment ago, I could feel myself taking up more and more space, and as of now, I reach a height midway up the trunk of a spruce. Now, I try to enjoy the weather, but am worried about the wind and the strength at which it will hit me. I can watch the grass in the field and hope the blades do not bend my way. I can listen to the trees and hope sound does not fly through the branches. I can worry and keep watch over all the little signs that tell me the wind is coming, or I can watch the birds fly, notice my own surroundings and experience what it is I have.

A gray day. October days. The time of day is anywhere between early morning and late afternoon. I look around and notice I am the only one. The sounds of birds in the trees and in the sky; they fly south, as they too know that it is time to go. All the signs of the end of the year are visible. All vegetation, amber and rust, making room for what will be in spring, and I begin to wonder about my location. Are there other places just like this one, or am

I completely alone? And suddenly, as if a stone had fallen from the sky and landed on top of me, I realize that I am, in every way, alone.

I take notice of the tall grass, not yet dead from the weather, and I watch it bend to one direction. I feel myself rustling in the light wind. And the fear returns, and I wonder, alone in this open field, how far can I spread myself. And I see, from my side, I see a single strand get taken by the wind, further up into the sky and falling to the ground. No longer a part of me, I watch it disappear into the distance. I begin to shake, and the more I shake, the more strands get pulled from the top of myself. One by one, they begin to be pushed off by the wind. I can now, after such a short amount of time, feel myself becoming smaller. With each passing minute. Before I can understand the full extent of my problem, the wind has become stronger. It is no longer single strands being taken from me, but patches. There is nothing I can do to fight back the wind. I can not struggle, but only watch as I spread across the open field.

And there, in an empty, cold field, the wind has taken away the haystack, bit by bit until there is nothing left.

THE RAILWAY

It was a somber evening as the sun gave the last efforts to gleam over the area. Treana had only then realized that she needed to step outside and follow the road to a stream where she used to sit as a child. Earlier in the day, she ended a romantic relationship, as she did not see a future with the man she had been spending so much of her time with. As she reflected on her past, she wished to continue her walk, following the stream until it parted ways from the path. The sun, now hardly giving any light, let the moon dominate the light source, which led Treana on a moonlit path that led to a set of train tracks that seemed to have been abandoned, as they were being eaten and taken over by shrubs and weeds. The wooden railway ties had cracked, but still supported the two rails that ran side by side as far as Treana could see. She stepped onto one of the railway ties and then onto another, as she strayed away from the original path and onto another.

She continued to be reminded of her failed relationship while searching through her thoughts. She looked for answers in hopes she would find comfort in her decision as she continued to walk down the tracks. She paused, took in the light of the moon, and gazed forward as far as she could see. She noticed that the two steel rail beams that the railway ties were holding in place, though separated where she stood, seemed to connect in the distance. In hopes of reaching the point where the two beams connected, she continued her walk in the direction she began. With her thoughts .never straying too far from the day's earlier events, she found herself quickening her pace, nearly running and passing each rectangular tie. Her eyes were no longer focused forward to where the beams appeared to be connected, but more to the ground, watching each step she took to keep her balance. After Treana felt she had run far enough, she began to slow her pace. Her breathing heightened, and eventually coming to a complete stop in the middle of the train tracks, she held herself still. When she regained her normal breathing rate, she looked up to see that she had not come any closer to where the two beams appeared to be connected. She then looked behind herself and noticed that the two beams appeared to be connected from where she had come from—but she knew that was not the case, and only the distance gave the illusion that they were ever connected to begin with. She knew, no matter how long she walked along the tracks, the rails would never meet. Though looking forward and behind gave the appearance of a union, it was where she stood that was the truth of where the two beams would forever sit.

THE PRISON

Carchar awoke in a narrow bed, his bare feet hanging over one end. He inspected the sheets, noticing they were not his usual ones. They were thin and smelled like cheap plastic. The pillow casing was similar to the sheets and wrapped in blue cotton. The rectangular mattress could hardly withstand the night, as Carchar could feel each individual coil spring piercing through the top and the sides. He could tell that he had slept well past noon, but the light that drifted into the room from the window did not indicate it could be anything but early morning. He pulled the sheets away and stepped onto the floor, where he was stunned to feel with his bare feet the rough and jagged stone that seemed to cover the ground. In complete confusion about where he could be, he did not begin to question himself, as even a question would give him a start on where and how to think. He sat back down on the bed and ran through his mind every action he committed the night before. He mumbled silently to himself until he came to the conclusion that he must have committed some kind of act of violence in his sleep. *But what kind of cell is this?* he thought. He then looked around, and a sudden fear fell upon him when he realized there didn't seem to be a door leading in or out of the room. There were only the four walls and a ceiling that seemed to be extraordinarily high above him. He thought, *Maybe they have dropped me from the ceiling or built these walls around me while I slept. Surely,* he thought, *surely this is some kind of game being played.* He could not think for a moment of anyone one who could commit such a cruel antic. He stood back up and slowly made his way to the window. His eyes came level to the windowsill, and he could hardly see out. He could see the bright blue sky, a few birds and green hills, but he did not recognize the area and therefore assumed that he was far from home, in the countryside or in another state altogether. He tried to pull himself up to the window, but the frame being as narrow as it was, made this pointless as he could not fit through, and the glass seemed to be too thick to push out. He figured if he found himself inside, there had to be a way one would enter, and therefore a way to exit.

He gave up on the window, realizing its only use was to shed some light in the room. He looked to each corner, realizing there was nothing but the narrow bed he had woken from, a glass bottle of water and a framed picture too high above the window for him to view. His confusion grew as he stood still. With nothing for him to put together, no reason or clue, he had nowhere to start his thinking, nowhere to begin a string of thought.

As his eyes leapt from one corner to the next, he noticed something strange in the walls. He could tell all four walls were made of brick, but the bricks appeared to have odd designs, many with pieces chipped away. He walked towards one wall to get a closer look in hopes of finding a loose brick. But as he got a closer look, he could see it was not a natural design or wear on the bricks, but purposeful carvings. The longer he inspected each brick, the more he noticed the words carved into each one. Within each brick was carved the title of a book Carchar had read, the title of a play he had seen, an article from the town paper or the title of a piece of music he had heard. Every brick that made up the wall had a title carved into the surface. Everything he had ever read or listened to, from what he could remember, had been carved into the wall.

Carchar backed away from the wall and walked to the one opposite. There, he viewed the bricks, but these did not have the titles of books or plays; each one had the name of a person he had met. Some he had forgotten, but many he remembered. From teachers to family to people he had only spoken to once before. A stranger then, but he must have had some conversation with each name on each brick at some point in his life.

He then went toward the wall his bed had been pushed up against. He climbed upon the bed and stood there, inspecting each brick and realizing that they too had been carved. This wall had everywhere he had ever been. Each brick had a street name or an address, a city or town, a dining room or an office number—everywhere Carchar had ever stepped foot had been covered.

He stood there on the bed wondering who could have done all of this, who could have known so much about him to build such a place. Three of the four walls were covered in information only he could know, even information he had long forgotten. The only wall that had nothing carved was the one with the window and the framed picture. From where he stood on the bed, he could see the outside clearly. A vacant landscape that stretched for miles. He thought about the location, as the room he resided in seemed to be out of place. And the more he thought about the situation, the more he wanted out. But with no exit nor door, and a window too small to push through, Carchar did not know where to begin. As he stood on the bed, he could see the framed picture that hung above the window—an oil painting, in dark gray colors, of the outside of the small room in which he had been placed. The oils on the canvas reflected all he owned and everything that had made him, and kept him, and all the things that had consumed, and would, in time, ruin him.

THE PAINTER

Siliga Pagota spent his schooldays alone with an easel, coloring over canvases with oil and water paints. He had developed a skill for the art at a young age, and though many had noticed his visible talent, it was never recognized beyond an idle skill. Siliga tried to display his work on the walls of his father's house, but the next day, they would all be removed and placed back in the room with the easel. The extent to which Siliga worked did not produce any reaction from those from whom he requested support. His father worked at a specialist firm in investment banking and had hopes of his son following a similar path.

As the years moved on, Siliga found himself painting less and less, until the canvases had concluded altogether. Years had washed away his work as he moved into studying the trades of his father. He had been set up in an office that overlooked the polluted city, and there he would spend most of his day, and often nights, in front of piles of papers that never had a bottom.

In the attic of the family house sat Siliga's portraits and landscapes. Stacked one by one, no light had been shed on the paintings in so many years. Left to gather dust, home for spiders and mice, and kept to be forgotten under hours and hours of banking. The paints had lost their smell, and the colors had faded. Some had noticeable tears from one corner to another. Unmoving, painted eyes watched in the dark and would never see the light again. Cabins that would never be visited. Forests with trails that would never be walked upon. Night skies with stars that had long faded away—so many intentions with no conclusion. Within each and every painting rested Siliga's young ambitions. Though he had often thought about picking up his brushes again, in his later years, he had found no use, no practical function in doing so.

At the end of each year, the firm Siliga worked for took the employees to an event involving equestrian sports. A small group of employees would sit in the stands and watch ban'ei racing while smoking cigars and talking over business matters. It had been a long year for the business, and as it seemed, another long year was ahead. Everything had been planned, and everyone was to remain where they were in their employment. Of course, Siliga knew how little chance he had to move up in the company and had lost all interest in where his life was heading. He stood up, stepped down from the stands and walked over to the stables where they kept the racehorses.

A man in checkered clothing and large black boots was sitting in the corner of a stable, polishing a thin skullcap helmet. He had been getting ready for a race when Siliga sat beside him.

"Is that your horse?" Siliga asked the small man polishing his shoes.

"That is her!" he replied with confidence.

Siliga commented on the beauty and size of the horse, and as they conversed, Siliga noticed the horse had one of its hind legs tied with a rope that attached to a railway pike plunged into the dirt ground. The horse stood still in the open stable and remained calm.

"Surely," said Siliga, "that spike in the ground is not what is holding that horse in place. I, myself, could pull it from the ground if I wished."

"Yes," replied the man, putting his boots on the ground. "Indeed, that spike is all that is keeping that horse tied down. You see," he continued to explain, "when the horse is only a colt, it does try to break itself loose, but at such a young age, it cannot free itself from the spike. It continues to try for weeks to escape, but without success. After less than a year, it gives up completely—and so, when it grows to be an adult, it still believes it can not escape, so it does not try."

THE SHATTERED HOUSE

It buzzed up and down, slamming its body against the glass window of the pickup truck. He watched it continuously try to break through the glass and escape to the outside. His foot pushed down on the gas, his eyes focused ahead; there was nothing he could do to stop this from happening. He could no longer see the wooden, busted door falling off the hinges, letting the insects come and go as they wished. As he continued to drive down the dirt road, he couldn't remember if he was coming or going. Had he already picked up what he set out to obtain? Once it sat in his trunk, his nerves would become calm, rest assured, and safe for one more night. Brown paper bag, Christmas wrapping paper holding the gift of escapism and so much less, and less the more it is taken.

After he visited the only store he was recognized in, he sat in his truck with the paper bag resting in his lap. The difficult part of the ordeal had concluded. He had what he needed to pass every hour of the night alone. The fly, still trapped in his truck, continued to try and get out, still bouncing off the window and frantically bouncing up and down, side to side.

The man dropped the plastic bottle out of the brown paper bag and into his dirty opened palm. He unscrewed the top, and without thought, began to pour the substance down his throat. He took in a long breath before pulling the truck away from the all-night drugstore and moved back in the direction of the shattered home he had lost sight of years earlier. There was no going back to the days when he felt productive in his work. Those past days led him to this—a house with shattered mirrors. The lights had used their fuse and had not been switched on in years. The windows had cracked, the wooden floors creaked and the ceiling leaked, warping the floorboards. Flies buzzed around the kitchen sink, feeding off the leftovers from weeks earlier. The trash hadn't been taken out in months, and the whole house filled with used plastic bags, broken beer bottles and empty plastic containers that once held 40 percent freedom. Fast food chain logos stained the walls and kitchen countertops. The house was a corpse, decaying on the inside. The house wore a smell like an attire of old rags—a smell the man had gotten used to over time.

He sat on the used couch with his used bottle. An old television sat across the room; the four channels he received brought him his daily news. He never gave any attention to what flashed from the screen but used it for the noise. The sound gave him the illusion of never being alone.

He sipped from the bottle while staring at the flashing box. When he got hungry, he would pick up the phone and dial the nearest delivery chain. When he felt like doing anything else, he would get up off the couch and begin to clean, but because of his state, while cleaning one area, he would often make a bigger mess in another. Hours would pass, and he would give up on any chance of tidying the house. He would then move to another room and go through his old belongings. He pulled out manuscripts of unpublished work, sheets of music no one had ever heard, photos of him when he still had all his teeth and hair. Every night he would try and figure out what went wrong, where and when his life started down another road, when he had abandoned all inspiration and aspirations. He would try and put things together, over and over, but would never be able to understand why he did not succeed. He wondered if he failed because he did not try hard enough, or if there was not enough attention given over to his art. Over and over—side to side, but he never found an answer.

He wandered from room to room until he found himself in the kitchen. He looked out the window that sat above the sink full of unwashed dishes. Buzzing along the windowsill, a fly bounced off the glass. Up and down, side to side, smashing its tiny body into the clear glass. It landed, staring out into the open fields. It was trapped inside the decay and could never leave as it failed to see exactly what it was that separated him from the world it desired and the world that kept him trapped in the corrosion.

ANIMALS

SYNTHETIC

Take one capsule by mouth. Take two capsules, crush, and press into a temperate liquid—then squeeze it into the U-100. Fill five cubic centimeters of the one hundred units. Absorb 1cc of blood into the cylinder to confirm the target—this is called red-flagging. *Do not consume alcoholic beverages while consuming this medicine.* A shot-glass, 375 ml in size, 40% venom, sits, sealed with the threatening label "Break in Case of Emergency". All the warning signs on a prescription bottle are directions for the addict on how to consume. *May cause drowsiness or dizziness.* May cause comfort or relief.

WARNING: Do not exceed the recommended dosage. Exceeding maximum recommended dosage may result in…

It is just like the first sign of consciousness, crumpling bed sheets and the moment between reality and the dreams that creep away. It's just like a wind pounding on the windowpane and what is left from the rain the night before. It is the smell of something light and sweet. *April is the coldest month. Life in dull roots—the spring rain,*[1] it's just like a song sung in open verse, *lilacs hidden in bud.* And maybe it's just like stepping on wooden panels that look out on the front acres that open like the cover of an exhausted Old Testament. Particles produce in the rays of the morning sun, and it is just like the first drag of a cigarette, and the sound of a green lighter striking back to initiate fire—its only objective. One

---

1   See T.S. Eliot, *The Waste Land.*

chemical reaction after another, until the annoyed lungs spit the skulled horses that trample the morning sky. Higher and higher, until they disappear. It's just like the dogs that converse with the flying shadows in the fields, chasing the tails of the pectoral sandpiper. Though only shadows, ignorant of what is real, they are satisfied—like dancing shadows in Plato's cave, they are satisfied. In the distance, the whistle of burning coal, across the tracks sown into the earth, and the sound of rolling lumber, repeating tasks, crippling and tightening around the steel—it'll be just like that. Like that open palm to receive the morning newspaper from the bicyclist in the wine-red golf shirt, it's just like that. A cigarette half smoked. Early penny loafers with creases where the toes bend. The distant sounds of fuels burning away the membrane. And in a potted plant, a spider. A web wrapped with white thin pearl, the artist unaware of what has been expressed overnight. Drops of rain between the lines of the maze, softly organized as visual imagination, but it remains a way of survival to its creator.

Burning lips at the edge of the yellow cylinder, inhale and inhale the last of the dizzy molecules, and then placed under the sole of the shoe to end the first page of *the morning*, to skip the awareness, sensitivity and reaction—it's just like that. As an assurance, the moment before darkness, it's just like warmth. And as is the morning, it is not, but as the mind enveloped in the act itself. It's just like that. It is just like that.

LA TRISTESSE DURERA TOUJOURS

With everything that has ever been accomplished, she finds herself balancing, eclipsing both unimaginable and unprecedented acts of artistry. The way she holds her eyes from corner to corner, a constant, refined rest that ropes in responses of affection. All the stars in all the nights, the swirls that spark atop the church steeple; she captures the attention of a room full of strangers, and still—still, she has once said and believed, *I am not valued to be treated kindly.* And though she has the right to the world, she unites with the myth she beats to heart. She takes her time with every word strung together and wrapped around her throat—they are shown as subtle stones that splash along every sentence. And she believes, watching the sunflowers grow, *I am no more valued to be treated kindly.*

And though she believes *great love carries the seeds of great sorrow*, she has become tired of wasting adoration on those who presumed it to be their own by right. More likely the work of the bard, she is the inspiration in the world of the arts. To muse idly by the flowerpots that blend in yellow and green. Few feelings left unfinished, she parades no mask, but only a stainless canvas that she pours over affections that shade in blue and gray. The flowers, they are people, and they stem across the café terrace at night. Acts of artistry, with everything that has ever been accomplished, the corners of her eyes, with all the stars that swirl at night, to be treated with the aptness of her smile alone.

She repeats, watching the sunflowers rise and rise, watching the sunflowers rise, she repeats, "this can last forever," and "this will last forever."

TENDING RABBITS[2]

It is going to be a long night. To be honest, I get to bed early—that is, early in the morning. And then it starts at work, and by work, I mean a bar named *Work*, not a place of employment. And there sit the clumsy ones with their glasses to their chins. And there are the smiles in half-skirts that flirt in braids and bells. Tips for nothing, putting back what was given in—they are the ghosts that pass between the glasses that hold a poison that never lasts.

But my breaks are the books that rest on shelves. After the hours, they call "after hours," a cigarette lasts the drive home. And there begins the conversations. It starts with a splash, a drip of something too fatal to consciousness in a glass of cranberry juice. And the creeping voices on the shelves call between their pages. And before the third glass is finished, I find myself leaving with Eliot, him and I. It is true, we agree, August is a much crueler month than April. But it doesn't last long, and before I speak, he is gone. And I move on, I move on, past the pages that belong in hands that do not shake. It is going to be a long night. It is going to be an early morning. I would fight with Marlowe, but I find him an ass, and I am sure Faust would feel the same. Now I have Goethe laughing and young Werther gasping, and I have only cracked the second bottle of—merlot?

---

2   *See* Of Mice and Men. John Steinbeck. *Pascal Covici*. 1937.

The smoke is so thick it could slow a flying brick, while the room rocks like pendulums in clocks that never tell time, but chime every time the glass needs company.

So I sit and wait. And I wait for that moment when I lose all touch with all sentiments—and applaud the loss of remorse. So I tap and I tap on a typewriter with calloused fingertips and wonder, *as happens sometimes, a moment settled and hovered and remained for much more than a moment.* And I say, dammit, Steinbeck! It is going to be an early morning. It is going to be a night full of everything empty. If you are able to count to ten and hold yourself to a single bottle of red, then you are a better man than I. But I have never been one for comparisons. And it is getting easier to tell the difference between Marlboro and Lucky Strike.

The bottles of red rabbit, stacked in a closet, another one opened and another one poured, and another one racing across the cigarette-stained floor. I have my reasons, and I have my cares, though neither have a reason to care for anything at all. So let me tend the rabbits, George, let us live off the land and find that dream you spoke of in dreams where all the things sound like melodies, and we can forget all that we have done.

Everything has only begun, and it doesn't stop until everything is dark and memory becomes a thing forgotten. As it often begins, the day before last, and before that. Depending on your perspective of things, it is either going to be a very late night or a very early morning.

THE AMETHYST IN KAE

The tan lines on her ring finger remind her of what she once admired desperately. Something that could never be touched or harmed by another or replaced by something less than the whole world. Now, collecting dust, the amethyst stone compiles no more memories, and the only thing she owns that tells stories is inside a box she dares to open in the company of strangers. Even alone, her memory dares to repeat the days she expressed emotion, but rather, every damaged moment that lasted a fraction of what was guarded in reality. She casts her eyes on a canvas covered in purity, but only gives attention to the tear in the corner. Nothing can be held to expectation when expectation climbs the back of fairy tales. And then again, she asks if this is new, the victim role she plays so well—if one believes her stories. She knows her lies too well and hands them out in a room full of the family she claims to despise behind closed doors. No fault of her own, she still sees herself as something no one would take her for.

She gave away all purpose and aspirations to gain less than ordinary, and she views it, at the time being, as a step forward—when in view of the situation, it is what she had always had in the past. She returned to the screen and someone alike. She forgot the dream and went back to comfort. Her egotistic screen shots amount to a thousand a day as she asks only of others, "Am I pretty?" and, "Am I pretty?"

And as time moves on, her looks as well, the attention she once received miserly will vanish and dispel. When there are no more hearts to break and all the moments flown. When she receives what she has sown, narrow and alone, the last heart she will ever break will be her own.

A transformation would show the deceiver inside her, as no victim ever goes back on their word. Lies worded so carefully, they echo little truth—just enough for her to accept what she tells herself. As she repeats, "I do this for me," she repeats, and she repeats, but little does she see, everything inside will start to bleed. And as it proceeds everyone will see, when she repeats, "I do this for me," there is no room left for those she needs. Time will pass, and will pass, all things will fade as they have. She lives only for herself, and in the end, she will find, that is all she has.

And when she receives what she has sown, narrow and alone, the last heart she will ever break will be her own.

TILL HUMAN VOICES WAKE US[3]

A million eyes watch a million eyes, and we are weak. Too weak. But it repeats, like a heartbeat that will not quit, it repeats. Like a heartbeat. Repeats—and you left me never the same. And by the way, what did the J. stand for, Eliot? Are we supposed to ask about the beautiful, or leave it as it is? And it is beautiful. So put your hand in mine, and let me take you to the place you were a child—just for a while, let us be children again. And of course, J. There will be time to wonder, "Do I dare," and, "Do I dare?" We are now in the same boat, you and I, we did together go. Whatever did you do, J? Did you ask? Or did you pass by Michelangelo in the deepest part of a night? Did you crawl along the bottom of the shore—with a million eyes watching a million eyes? I have to wonder, "Do I dare?" I will not grow any older and refuse to not say what I mean. And the most important question you asked, J, "Would it have been worth it, after all?" After all, it repeats like a heartbeat, is it going to be worth walking in crutches, punches to the moral code of all that is holy in heaven? No, no, we are not the prince of Denmark, but we are neither the ghost. So let us go, let us go, and God, will you let us go? Etherized, it is true, J. You said it so well, and you have never said it better. A poem like a letter to a lover that is bitter, we are tethered to the hapless, and once

---

3   Eliot, T.S. *The Love Song of J. Alfred Prufrock. Magazine, 1915, Herriet Monroe Chapbook* (1917). The Egoist, Ltd. United States. June 1915. As a homage to Prufrock, seclusion, and maybe something else.

we remember, there is nothing so much better than the feeling ever after.

So let us go, you and I, and let us repeat like a heartbeat, down a half-deserted street—and it is true, we are too damn weak. Do I dare have her hold me in her arms with all the marks of all the stars, all the tears and all the scars, all the flaws she knows too well? A million eyes watching a million eyes. And J., how did you end? Is it true, she didn't mean anything at all? Do you still sit alone with your tea on your throne, your face with a groan—alone and alone? We are stubborn, it is true, we are weak through and through, but is it any better with or without? We are poets, no doubt, but bastards, for sure—so we can dream, because I too will never ask. You and I, let us go, and repeat like a heartbeat, swollen and weak, crippled and bleak—till human voices wake us, let us drown in what we do to ourselves. Let our shoelaces tangle in what we have done to keep us from walking. Till human voices wake us, let us be alone due to a stubborn heart, and a weak beat that will forever repeat.

UNDERSTANDABLE, FLAMMABLE ANIMALS

Of course, Leopold Bloom is a dreaded name in English literature, but to some, myself not one, it is as good a name as Carraway. If my qualms lay anywhere, it is not with Joyce, but those that are able to find meaning outside the single page of action. It does scratch at the back on my neck, every word trekked along a page that served no purpose but to comfort a stream of consciousness that would not exist, but for an unwittingly bored man and his pen. Let it forget. Let it run, on and on. Here, there is no conventional transition. Here, there is only Joyce—and that is the way it was supposed to run. From time to time, one may mirror such a phenomenon as stream of consciousness. After all, what is life if not freewriting? Step after step, no transition from day to day—the long unwinding mind of god.

And imagination, the most powerful natural sleeping aid. Imagine this stream leads to an ocean of value and not a barren, desolate catacomb. This consciousness rivers toward Eden, and far past imagination. If you argue with yourself long enough, you too can sleep at night. Far past imagination—far past anything imagined. Occasionally, one may trip into the common tropes of a genre that rests between mythology and nursery rhymes. Poetry is better off dead, and there is nothing left to go on about but the actions human beings and other grotesque things share in ruination. Believe them to be beasts and fowls. Appetites and thoughts—the constant struggle between starvation and indulging—less thought, more appetite. Piles of words, scrambled, fried, rigorously applied, forgotten and confined to four walls where one hides their truths and lies—their laughs, their cries. It becomes easy to relate to self. Self to unconscious self. Self to else—and repeat myths and rhymes. Conscious dreaming, line after line, understandable—too far gone.

Bloom rests easy knowing daisies never bloom. Him, having the advantages others were not given, he does not criticize—but is criticized. It is true: Leopold is a dreaded name in English literature. But one should not be critical of others, as any father would tell you—appetites intrude. Intrude. Exclude a symbolic father—four o'clock rendezvous—but enough of Homer—less of Odysseus—more of trouble.

And imagination, the most powerful, natural stimulate. Powdered imagination. Lines crossed, tied and bound. Freudian advice to never take no as an answer. Anything can be set on fire in one's own head. Putting it through the agonizing task of storytelling is left to those tied and bound. No is an anesthetic. Freudian advice and powdered imagination.

But if one takes away the flow of random thought, one will put together the animal as such: Bloom finally leaves his house—welcomes Boylan. Stephen goes about his day. They find themselves at St. Maternity's Hospital. The enemy, conscious—the hero, compassion. The end. Let Molly dream. These are animals. There are no such things as tamed, focused fires.

PLASTIC SHEETS

There was sometimes a light on in his head. As he watched the clouds roll through the skies from the window of the hospital, he counted the days wasted and wasted on the plastic sheets. There was sometimes a shiver in his left hand. He listened to the footsteps rushing outside his door while remembering the music he listened to as a child. There was nothing left to do but remember—though there wasn't much to remember but morning infirmity, cloudy nights. Nothing left but the sound of footsteps outside his door.

Printed in Canada